FRAGILE THINGS

folkestone sins

FRAGILE THINGS

FOLKESTONE SINS BOOK ONE

SAMANTHA LOVELOCK

Cover Design by LJDesigns

Editing by Brandi Zelenka

Ebook ISBN 978-1-7772534-1-7

Print ISBN 978-1-7772534-0-0

For my Mum. You're my hero. Thank you for being there every single day, even when things got dark. I love you more than I can ever express.

and

For Brad, my very own second chance romance. Seventeen seems like forever ago, but somehow I always knew it was you. Thank you for changing my life.

CONTENTS

I was innocent once, but I didn't get to stay that way for long. Raised by a single mother somewhere in the vicinity of upper-lower class, day-to-day life was always a struggle. My mom tried to cover it with her flowing Bohemian skirts and shimmery laughter, but even my youngest self knew something wasn't right. Secrets haunted her like misty ghosts; she carried them in the slump of her shoulders and the depths of her sea glass colored eyes.

Over the years, her boyfriends would come and go, but none of them were around for longer than a few months. Her parents were gone, and my father was nothing more than a one-night stand. The only constant was us, and in my tiny world, she was my best friend, my safe harbor, and my favorite person. I would have done anything, given anything, to keep her with me forever.

Right up until the day the darkness swallowed her whole, and she left me all alone.

CHAPTER ONE

STELLA

The constant banging echoes with a heavy foreboding that drags me awake. Cursing under my breath, my legs tangle in the sheets in my hurry to get up and I fall back onto the bed, setting the less than sturdy frame shaking and squeaking.

It is far too early for this.

Lying flat on my back, I squeeze my eyes shut and count to ten, willing whoever is at my door to go away. When that doesn't work, I grind my teeth in frustration and roll off my slightly swaybacked mattress. Thoroughly annoyed now and my eyes still blurry with sleep, I stumble my way toward the noise while yanking my T-shirt and sleep shorts out of the cracks and crevices they crawled into while I slept.

"There'd better be something on fire, asshole!" I yell toward the locked and dead-bolted door from the middle of my puny living room. At the sound of my voice, the banging starts in earnest. "For fuck's sake, I'm coming!" Peering through the scuffed up peephole, I'm not exactly overjoyed to see the lecherous leer of my infinitely skeevy landlord on

3

the other side. Flicking the locks and opening the door just wide enough with one hand, I instinctively cross the other arm over my thin shirt to keep him from eye-groping my tits.

"What the hell do you want at six o'clock in the morning, Todd?" A sizable yawn escapes me, and since I'm more concerned with covering my chest than covering my mouth, he winces as my breath floats in his direction. I don't even try to stifle my satisfied grin; this fucker's roving eyes and grabby hands deserve far worse than a little dragon breath.

He doesn't say a word, just stands there, staring at me.

"Earth to Todd. Make a damn sound already. Silently ogling me this early in the morning is more aggravating than usual." It's repulsive to me that I have to be even marginally civil to this guy when all I want to do is junk punch him. Unfortunately, there aren't many landlords in this town willing to rent to an underage girl with no credit history, so I have to play nice. Ish.

His small, close-set eyes—somewhere between baby shit brown and dirty old mustard—lazily make their way from my shapely bare legs up to my heart-shaped, and currently very fucking irritated face. Licking his slimy lips, he half-chuckles, and it sounds like a death rattle.

"This came for you. Ran into the delivery guy yesterday and told him I would make sure you got it." He lifts his scarecrow-thin arm, and, for the first time, I catch sight of the package gripped in his left hand. Wrapped in plain brown butchers' paper and about the size of a family-sized cracker box, I can see his greasy fingerprints all over it. Shuddering involuntarily, I reach forward, doing my best to grab it without having to touch his fingers in the process.

"How about you let the delivery guy do what he's paid to do?" I suggest, shaking my head in a mix of frustration and

4

disgust. Bored with his little game now, I slam and lock the door without another word. My need to make sure he actually leaves has me checking the peephole, just in time to see his usual constipated expression morph into something darker, likely at not being thanked nicely.

Big deal. The guy's a card-carrying creeper, and there's only so much of him I can stomach.

The pockmarked hallway mirror on the way to the kitchen reveals a grumpy raccoon; last night's mascara and eyeliner now smeared around a pair of tired, deep violet-blue eyes. Dumping the package on my scarred kitchen table, I run the broadside of my index fingers under my eyes to wipe the black away and park my ass in my single, wobbly kitchen chair.

Pulling one leg up to my chest and resting my chin on my knee, I eyeball the package in front of me. The longer I sit staring at it, the more my nerves hum, and the stronger my strange sense of foreboding gets. Who would send *me* anything? With no family to speak of and my deeply ingrained distrust of pretty much the entire human race, I have exactly one friend and a handful of acquaintances. I can't think that a single one of them would spring for the price of postage.

For two years, I've been on my own, ever since my mom up and disappeared the winter after I turned fifteen, and any small sense of normality in my life vanished with her. Now, two and a half years later, I have developed a finely honed sense of when things are about to go sideways.

Today is starting to feel *exceptionally* sideways.

With a resigned sigh, I slide the package toward me to get a closer look.

I shake it a little.

Give it a suspicious sniff.

5

Set it back down.

Nibbling on my left thumbnail, my go-to bad habit when I'm overthinking, I contemplate the grease-stained wrapping a little longer. Finally, curiosity overtakes wariness, so I pick up the package again and rip it open.

To my utter surprise, nestled inside the cardboard shell is a wooden box, carved with a small cluster of vines and what looks like dainty sparkling stars. Polished to a warm cinnamon sheen, it's just big enough to hold a large paperback novel. After turning it over a few times and running my hands over its understated beauty, my fingertips find the small latch on the front and press open the hinged lid. Honestly, I have no idea what I expect to see inside. I *can* say with utmost certainty, however, that the little ecru envelope with fancy black cursive script spelling out *Stella Evangeline Bradleigh* wasn't on the list of possibilities.

Resisting the urge to drop the box like it bit me, I gingerly set it, still open, on the table with shaking hands. My wooden chair creaks in protest as I lean back, taking a few deep breaths to try to quiet the panic that surges through me like a rogue wave at the sight of my real name.

The name nobody is supposed to know.

Up until my fifteenth birthday, I was Evvie Ellis. Stubborn. Intelligent. Creative. I may have been from the wrong side of the proverbial tracks, but my mom and I did the best we could, and for the most part, I was happy.

There have always been strange gaps in time that were dark voids in my mind, but Mom told me it was because I was too busy remembering the good things, so there was no room for anything else. She would get this weird deer in headlights look and start to cry when I would tell her I wanted to try to fill in some of the holes in my Swiss cheese memory, so I learned to shove my questions and fears down deep.

Her tendency for avoidance decided to bite me in the ass the night I turned fifteen.

Over store-bought chocolate birthday cake and melting vanilla ice cream, my mother lost her mind. At least that's the only explanation I could think of at the time. Playing with a loose thread on the edge of her sleeve, and unable to meet my eyes, she told me a story about a baby named Stella Evangeline Bradleigh. A baby who was supposedly me, born in a town she refused to name, far from where we lived in Gloversville, NY. Grabbing my face desperately with both hands, she made me promise over and over to never tell anybody who I really was, not letting go until I said the actual words. Finally satisfied, she patted my cheek and told me I would always be safe as long as I kept my promise.

Like flipping a switch, she went back to her cake and ice cream, smiling and humming softly to herself as she ate while I stared at her, bewildered, and wondering what just happened.

She never spoke of it again. I was too afraid of what else she might say if I asked, so like everything else dark and scary in my life, I jammed it into a closet somewhere in the back of my mind.

Looking back, that was a colossally stupid move. The fear and doubt she left with me that night have colored nearly every minute of the almost three years since. Had I known my mother would disappear on me a few months later, I would have pushed for answers, no matter how awful they might have been.

When my friends found out she was gone, somebody's

parents called Child Protective Services. I was motherless, fatherless, and had no other relatives to speak of, so it all ended on a quiet Tuesday morning. With nobody stepping up to take me in, I said goodbye to everything I knew. Filling a black garbage bag with my things, I became just another cog in the foster system machine.

I lasted four and a half months before I ran.

Sleeping through the night is a trick I've never mastered, and being trapped in this hellhole of a group home doesn't make me inclined to figure it out. The fears that whisper during my waking hours here are ten times louder in the dark of night.

Lights out was hours ago, but I'd only managed to doze off fitfully, every car that passed outside my window and every dog that barked in the distance jarring me back to my shitty reality.

Hearing the soft shuffling sounds too late to defend myself, I'm powerless to stop the hand that snakes out, gripping a handful of my long, thick hair by the roots and scraping short jagged nails roughly along my scalp. Dragged head-first out of bed, I land awkwardly on my back. Squinting through the near-perfect darkness and stinging pain in my scalp, my watering eyes can barely make out the doughy, round face of my latest nightmare before her fat fist lands, with full force, square in my stomach.

With the wind knocked out of me, there is nothing I can do except curl into a tiny ball on the dirty floor in a vain attempt to protect myself as blows mercilessly rain down on my face and torso. Grabbing for my hair again, she yanks my head back with one hand, her other landing a shot to my nose with a sickening crunch that has hot coppery blood flooding down my face and into my gasping mouth. The metallic scent seems to appease the junior sociopath because she climbs off me and slowly backs away.

Before my punch-drunk brain can figure out how to get up, I catch a hard kick to my mid-back that knocks the wind from my lungs again, and that's when I realize she must've brought friends. A few well-placed ratty sneaker kicks to my back and stomach later, they raise a collective snicker and slut-sneeze their way out of my room.

Finally left alone, I lie on the peeling linoleum, listening to my nose gurgle, broken bits of time floating back to me.

Pieces of me that don't quite fit together anymore.

With adrenaline still pumping through my veins, panic starts to follow, so I begin counting slowly backward from one hundred. Somewhere around thirty-five or so, my breathing returns to a more regular rhythm and my nose stops actively gushing. Heaving myself up, I stagger like a drunken prom queen to the windowless bathroom at the end of the hall. Not wanting to even glance at my mashed up face in the mirror, I bend over the small toilet and retch until there's nothing left.

After cleaning myself up as best I can and shutting off the bathroom light, I quietly shuffle my way back to my assigned room. Grabbing a handful of cheap tissues from the box beside my bed, I drop them on the blood-dotted floor and use my feet to wipe up as much as I can. Kicking the resulting reddened mess into the corner of the room, I tell myself I'll clean it up properly in the morning.

Gingerly, I arrange my bruised body into a bearable position on my small single bed and stare at the ceiling until morning.

Fighting my way back to the present, I stand on rubbery knees and retrieve my relatively ancient iPhone from beside my bed. The catalog of music stored on it is extensive. I settle on Thom Yorke's 'Hearing Damage', plopping the phone on the kitchen table in hopes of finding some calm within the ebb and flow of notes.

When I was tiny, my mom introduced me to music as if it were a living, breathing creature that twined around your ankles and crawled under your skin. I learned to hear in color, and every person I've met and every experience I've had has become a part of my soundtrack.

The urge to crawl back under the covers is strong, but I force myself to sit down. Reluctantly, I reach into the open wooden box for the pristine envelope that bears my full birth name. My finger slides under the back flap, and with my stomach crawling up my throat, I pull out a matte black business card and a folded sheet of paper made of the same expensive-looking stock as the envelope.

DEAREST STELLA,

I HOPE THIS FINDS YOU. THIS BOX BELONGED TO YOUR MOTHER, AND I THOUGHT IT SHOULD BE YOURS NOW. THOUGH IT HAS TAKEN ME YEARS TO FIND YOU, PLEASE KNOW IT WASN'T FOR LACK OF TRYING. YOUR MOTHER MADE THE CHOICE A LONG TIME AGO TO LEAVE, AND SHE KEPT YOU BOTH VERY WELL HIDDEN. YOU AND I ARE ALL THAT'S LEFT OF OUR FAMILY NOW.

I UNDERSTAND IF YOU WISH TO CONTINUE TO BE ON YOUR OWN, BUT I SINCERELY HOPE YOU WILL AT LEAST MEET WITH ME ONCE.

SHOULD YOU WANT TO MEET ME AND SEE WHERE YOU COME FROM, PLEASE CALL THE NUMBER ON THE ENCLOSED CARD AND THEY WILL ARRANGE A PLANE TICKET TO THE WEST COAST FOR YOU.

IF YOU CHOOSE NOT TO COME, KNOW THAT YOU ARE LOVED.

ALWAYS, AUNT CECILY

Flipping the letter over, I stare at the California address and phone number written on the back. Somehow I don't even notice the tears streaming down my face until they leave tiny wet dimples on the paper clutched in my fingers.

Giving in to the quiet sobs struggling to break free, I let the letter flutter to the floor as I wrap my arms around myself. As I try to calm my racing heart, one question echoes on repeat through my brain: I have an aunt?

After a mostly sleepless night spent questioning pretty much my entire existence, I make swift work of the three-block walk to The Juneberry the next morning. Pulling open the heavy back door of the popular local diner and stowing my purse in the tiny break room, I tie on my clean apron and give Sally a kiss on her round, flushed cheek as I walk through the kitchen.

The morning shift is one of my favorites. Busy, but not crazy, with most of the crowd consisting of blue-haired regulars and the occasional group of college kids looking to nurse their hangovers with a tasty, greasy breakfast.

When I found my way to Baldwinsville after running from the group home, it seemed like the perfect place to become invisible. Small enough to not be on any CPS radar, and just large enough to blend in. Sally, the tiny blonde diner-owning dynamo, took pity on my not quite sixteen-year-old self and gave me a job even though I was underage. A few months of washing dishes later, I graduated to waitressing.

People here know me as Stella, though I still use Ellis as my last name. I couldn't risk using my full birth name on the off chance my mother had been right about me being in danger, and I couldn't use the name she raised me with in case CPS was looking for me. So I settled on a combination of the two. An acquaintance with somewhat less than legit ties got me set up with a passable ID so I could at least open a bank account and register for online high school classes.

It's been just over two years now. Long enough for the old-fashioned Formica tables, red leather booths, and shiny chrome accents to seem cozy rather than corny, and for me to not be startled every time the bells over the entrance door cheerily announce a customer's coming or going.

The morning passes in a blur of friendly smiles and stacks of pancakes. Normally, I would consider it a successful start to the day. Still, the feeling that something isn't quite right is unshakable. Sort of like everything is ever so slightly out of focus or not quite the right color. Hoping it might just be a residual effect from last night's crappy sleep, I pull together a scrambled egg sandwich with some leftover bacon.

"Sal! I'm on break! Be back in fifteen!" I shout to be heard over silverware clattering against plates and the patchwork of conversation. Catching my eye from behind the counter, she gives me an understanding wink, knowing full well where I'm going.

Folding the sandwich into a square of paper towel, I leave out the back door. Mr. Ambrose, one of the older homeless men who rests his head back here in the alley each night, is waiting patiently for me. Bringing him something from the kitchen around the same time each day has become our routine. Leaning against the sun-warmed red bricks along the side of the building, he gratefully accepts his lunch and takes a bite, chewing thoughtfully.

"Why you lookin' so shook, girl?" he asks with his mouth full. I shrug one shoulder and smile ruefully.

"Didn't sleep well last night. A strange delivery had my mind working overtime." Lowering my eyes, I realize my brain is once again stewing over the questions raised by the beautiful wooden box and its unexpected contents. A few minutes of silence pass, and I can feel Mr. Ambrose staring at me. I lift my eyes to meet his piercing gaze.

"Girl, when somethin' gets that stuck in your craw, only one way to stop the sting. You gotta pull it out quick. These things gotta be faced. Stared at, straight in the eye, in the full light of day." With that, he tips his ragged plaid cap to me in thanks for his lunch and sets off down the alley, leaving me staring after him shaking my head.

Somehow his words hit home with me. I can't ignore that letter any more than I could an elephant on a trapeze. Something in me craves answers and connection more than it's afraid of them. With a sigh and increasingly sweaty palms, I venture back inside to tell Sally I'm going to need some time off.

CHAPTER TWO

STELLA

"*F*uckity, fuck fuck fuck." I know I must seem like a crazy person muttering profanity to myself, but right now, I couldn't care less. My head is pounding, and my anxiety is threatening to choke me outright.

It took me a full day, and at least thirty-two failed attempts before I convinced myself to call the number on the card and ask the agency to book the flight across the country. It took another half a day to force my fingers to text my arrival information to the number on the back of The Damn Box Letter. That's what I've started referring to it as—*The Damn Box Letter*. The thing that turned my whole life upside down. Again. My phone pinged back at me less than a minute later.

I'M SO HAPPY. SAFE TRAVELS. SEE YOU SOON.

Let me tell you, those three short sentences carried more weight than any others I'd ever read. We're talking leaden, bloated, sink to the bottom of the ocean kind of weight.

I'm headed to a town called Folkestone, California. Just north of San Francisco and just west of What the Fuck Was I Thinking. Having never left the confines of New York State, even figuring out what to take with me became a chore of comedic proportions.

To add insult to injury, I have a fear of flying I knew nothing about until now. By fear, I mean terror, and by terror, I mean the pants-shitting kind. The flight attendant had to practically drag me to my seat. After blindly managing to strap myself in, I offered up hastily worded prayers to every deity I could think of. Almost immediately, my leg developed a nervous tick all on its own. About an hour into the flight, my three-drinks-in seatmate leaned his heavily bearded, man-bun self over to me.

"Hey there, little girl, maybe you should stop with the leg thing. Don't want the other passengers thinking you know something about the plane that they don't," he slurred at me, winking sloppily and making small explosion sounds under his breath like a giant, hairy, seven-year-old.

"Hey, maybe you should mind your own fucking business and eat a dick," I shot back at him, flashing the sweetest, most saccharine smile I could manage while continuing to grit my teeth in terror. That seemed to dissuade him from any further commentary, and my asinine leg continued its shaking unchecked for the rest of the flight.

Now, as we make our descent into San Francisco International Airport, along with my insane muttering and shaky leg, my stomach is clenching, threatening to empty its contents into the lap of the asshole sitting beside me. Once the plane rolls to a full stop, I'm thinking the same flight attendant who dragged me onto the plane is going to need to carry me off of it, since all my bones feel like they've just turned to goo.

Fuck you, fear. This girl's got no time for you today.

Channeling my inner badass, I shove past my crushing anxiety and miraculously pull my shit together enough to exit the plane under my own steam.

Once in the terminal, I follow the rest of the herd to baggage claim to collect the hard-shell black suitcase Sally insisted I borrow. The screen above the carousel shows me I have some time to kill before the luggage from my flight is available. Scanning my surroundings for the nearest restroom, I spot one mostly hidden in a small alcove across the concourse. As I shift my weight from foot to foot, debating whether I should wait until I have my luggage or not, my frayed nerves really start to drive me nuts, and I know I need to find some chill fast.

Historically speaking, there are only two things that successfully relax me when I'm this wound up, and since I'm standing alone in the middle of a crowded airport, I opt for the less naked choice. Pulling out my phone, I shove my earbuds in, cranking up The Anix's 'Renegade' and letting the music flow through me like a balm as I dash for the ladies' room. When I find it empty, my bladder quivers in thanks.

This song is one of my favorites. I half sing, half hum along as I do my business and wash my hands, stopping to run my cool, wet fingers across the back of my neck before drying them. Tossing the wadded up paper towel into the trash can on my way out, I yank open the restroom door and walk face-first into a solid male chest. Strong hands reach out to steady my shoulders, and I'm instantly enveloped by the enticing scent of soft sandalwood and warm sunshine.

Quickly yanking out my earbuds, my brain registers that I'm eye-level with the black Vans logo emblazoned across the front of a well-fitting, snug, dark gray T-shirt. I'm afraid to look up, suddenly hyper aware of how close we're standing to each other. He must sense my reaction to his proximity because a small but profoundly sexy chuckle rumbles out of him. Slowly raking my gaze up his nicely defined chest, I stop to admire the gloriously intricate black and gray tattoo winding its way up his right arm, the way his shirt emphasizes his broad shoulders, and the faint throb of his pulse in the hollow of his throat.

Sighing softly, I lift my eyes further. A startlingly handsome face stares appreciatively down at me with cocky amusement. He's young, probably eighteen or nineteen, but they sure don't grow guys like this where I'm from. The corner of his lips tuck up in a little sideways grin, and his dark blue eyes gleam with mischief.

Well, shit. As they say in the movies, 'Mischief is my middle name.'

I don't know this guy from Adam, but then again, I don't know anybody here, so if there was ever a time to make out with a smokin' hot stranger, now would be it. That look in his eyes is a challenge if I've ever seen one, and I'm not one to walk away from a challenge, especially one that looks and smells this good. Raising slowly onto my tiptoes, I run the tip of my nose up the side of his warm, tanned throat while sliding my hands up his firm chest. I'm rewarded with his sharp intake of breath that tells me he wasn't expecting me to play along.

Grinning wickedly at my small victory, I graze my teeth along his sculpted jawline. His hands tightly squeeze my shoulders before one leaves its perch to trace lazily down my spine, and the other fists into the back of my long, glossy black hair. Pulling softly to force my chin up, it feels like he stares directly into my soul as he thoughtfully runs his tongue across his very kissable bottom lip. At that moment, I catch the slight glint of the stud piercing his tongue.

Good lord, I'm all in.

Feeling me strain lightly against the fist in my hair, he releases just enough for me to reach up and capture that bottom lip between my teeth before letting it slowly slide free.

The game is real now, and I've just upped the ante.

Growling low in his throat, he turns and flattens me up against the alcove wall, the hardness growing between his legs pressing against my hip. Wrapping his beautifully tattooed arm around my waist, he pulls me more tightly to him, tracing the seam of my lips with his velvet tongue before engulfing me in the hottest, most panty-melting kiss I have ever experienced.

Unfortunately, before I even have time to catch my breath, let alone fully enjoy the warmth of his lips, his back pocket starts to vibrate. He pulls away slightly, swearing under his breath as he reaches for his phone.

Startled back to reality, my face flushes faintly pink. I flash a cheeky grin before quickly disentangling myself from the gorgeous stranger's embrace and dart out of the alcove, heading toward the luggage carousel and not looking back.

Wow.

Wow wow.

That was intense and incredible and insane. I can't believe I was just brazen enough to make out with a total stranger. Realizing now that the entire thing happened without a word, I find myself wondering what his voice sounds like. A laugh tumbles out as I notice my nerves aren't quite as taut as they were.

Sex and music, my go-to magic anxiety relievers; thanks for your assistance, random hottie.

Absently nibbling on the inside of my cheek and deep in thought, I almost miss seeing my suitcase go by, the hot pink ribbon tied to the handle fluttering at me in greeting. My feet are moving before my brain fully engages, and I lunge forward, reaching awkwardly to snatch for my bag. My still-unsteady knees betray me, and I stumble into another passenger waiting for his own luggage. Throwing my arm out to catch myself before I fall over, my palm collides with a familiar chest, and his warm, steady grip closes around my wrist. Snatching my hand away without looking at his face, I slip through the crowd and move closer to the belt, managing to grab my bag on its second pass and feeling his eyes on me as I take off at a run.

Utterly overwhelmed by the past seventy-two hours and my little erotic interlude, I slow down once I'm out of his eyeline. Moving mindlessly with the crowd toward the arrivals waiting area, the echo of his tantalizing scent floats in the back of my mind.

The churning in my stomach starts up again in full force, though, as I scan the nameless faces in front of me. It hits me that I have no idea who I'm looking for.

None.

Zero.

Shit.

Just as I'm about to turn tail and find the quickest and cheapest way back to New York, a small white card held in a masculine but well-manicured hand catches my eye. *Miss Bradleigh* is written neatly on it in fine black marker. Putting away my phone, I take in the perfectly tailored black suit and the careful smile of the older man who belongs to the hand. By sheer force of will, I convince myself to move close enough for me to speak and be heard over the noise of loved ones greeting each other with familiarity and excitement.

"Uhm, hi. I'm Stella Bradleigh?" My voice breaks on the taste of the unfamiliar surname in my mouth, and the statement comes out sounding like a squeaky question.

"Good afternoon, Miss Bradleigh. I trust your flight was pleasant? The car is out front. Please follow me." His voice sounds just like he looks: efficient, smooth, and polished. Before I can reply—or even blink, really—he's already pried the suitcase handle out of my grip and is gliding his way swiftly through the massive number of people between us and the automatic doors leading outside. Since a substantial amount of my worldly possessions are crammed into that suitcase he's so effortlessly carrying, I get my ass moving in his direction. Sprinting, I finally manage to catch up with him just as the exit doors are sliding open. He must have forty years on me, yet I'm the winded one!

"Pretty spry for an old dude, huh?" I joke, my hands on my hips as I chuff and wheeze like an emphysemic buffalo, waiting for my lungs to re-inflate.

"Yes, Miss, spry indeed," he answers with a barely repressed grin. He takes my elbow gently and steers me toward the rear passenger side door of the glossy midnight blue Cadillac XTS.

After planting me in the backseat and tucking my bag neatly into the trunk of the car, Mr. Spry Fancy-pants slips behind the wheel and we're on our way. We pull smoothly into the line of vehicles leaving the airport heading north, and I keep my eyes trained on the water of the San Francisco Bay on my right, wondering for the zillionth time if I've made a massive mistake.

As we cross onto the island and drive past a discreet sign

for the Folkestone Yacht Club, I start to pay more attention to the small, exclusive town around us. The coastline still runs beside the car on one side, but now stunningly long driveways wind their way lazily up the other side to large houses perched on the hillside and nestled among majestic trees. My eyes devour the beauty of the landscape surrounding us, marveling at the dappled afternoon sunlight tracing lacy patterns over the streets.

"Spry, I'm a thousand percent sure this is some nasty joke, and I'm an idiot for falling for it," I manage to choke out around the lump of tears caught in my throat.

Tears now? What the hell? This whole situation is seriously fucking with my juju.

I don't cry over sentimental, pretty things. In fact, I don't cry much at all anymore. Catching my eyes in the rear-view mirror, the driver flashes me a small, reassuring smile.

"Don't worry, Miss Bradleigh. You'll do just fine." I don't remotely believe him, but there's no time to delve into the full breadth of my insecurities as we turn into a partially obscured driveway, and a pair of massive iron gates silently swing open. The house ahead comes into full view, and my throat tightens further at the grand estate before me.

As we roll to a gentle stop, I notice the lone willowy figure waiting in the wide welcoming entryway. Waiting, I assume, for me.

CHAPTER THREE

STELLA

Frozen in the backseat, I stare through the tinted side window in wide-eyed disbelief at the woman on the porch as panic starts to crawl across my skin with little spidery feet. Spry comes around to open my door, and when I make no move to leave the relative safety of the backseat, he reaches for my hand.

"I can't," I whisper, silently pleading with him to take me back to the airport, back to the hollow but relatively safe existence I knew.

He gently tugs me out of the car and gives my trembling fingers a small squeeze before moving to retrieve my bag. I stand motionless beside the car with my head lowered and force myself to remember how to breathe. The trunk closes with a soft click, and my head lifts in time to see my borrowed suitcase disappear into the house. Slowly, I follow it, making my way up the steps with my heart thudding in time with each footfall until I stand, pale and shaking, face-to-face with a ghost.

"Mom?" The word slips from my lips before I realize I've said anything. The woman shakes her head slightly in response, a deep sadness somehow apparent in that small movement.

The closer I look, the more the slight differences between them become clear. This woman is softer than I remember my mother being. Time and circumstance haven't been nearly as hard on her. The honey streaks in her beechnut hair add a warmth and depth that my mother could never have afforded, and though her eyes are the same shade of sea glass blue, the lines that frame them seem to be from laughter rather than tears.

Staring into those eyes, my whole body is wracked with violent tremors as the stress of the past couple of days finally catches up with me. Harsh, gasping sobs escape my lips, and I double over as my stomach makes good on the earlier threat of emptying its contents. The touch of a soft hand on my back, both familiar and unknown, pushes me entirely over the edge, and I collapse in an undignified puddle at her feet.

Lavender and gardenia. Such a pretty scent. Stretching with the fluidity and grace of a well-loved cat, I crack open an eyelid, and reality comes crashing back as I take in the unfamiliar surroundings.

"You could be her twin," I whisper. The woman in the pale turquoise wingback chair next to the bed raises her eyes from the novel in her hand and gives me a gentle smile.

"We used to hear that all the time when we were young, and believe me, there were times we took full advantage of it." Her smile deepens, remembering long-ago escapades. "My name is Cecily. Your mom, Catherine, was my big sister. I'm delighted to finally meet you, Stella." Pulling myself to a sitting position against the mountain of pillows behind me, I hesitantly reach out and shake the finely boned and beringed hand she offers me.

"The Damn Box Letter. You sent it." A statement, not a question. I wince at the crassness of it, instantly wanting to take it back.

"I did," she admits with a chuckle and a nod. "I wasn't sure what, if anything, you knew about me, so I thought that might be the least intrusive way of introducing myself. If you had no desire to meet me, you could just ignore the box and the letter and go on with your life."

Not likely.

She watches me with curiosity as I push myself out of the comfort of the pillow mountain and walk to the large window overlooking the mind-blowing landscape below. With trees for what looks like miles in every direction, interspersed with areas of lush green lawn, the property resembles something out of a movie. Closer to the house, an outdoor kitchen and sitting area flank a sparkling aqua swimming pool, complete with a grotto and small waterfall.

"What is this place?" I ask, without turning away from the window.

"This is Tweedvale Cottage." Her use of the word cottage elicits a bark of laughter from me, and she grins in return as she comes to stand beside me. "If you look to the left, past the patio, you can see the roofline through the trees. That's the original cottage. After the main house was built, the cottage was turned into a guest house by your grandparents," she explains, pointing to a small outbuilding barely visible through the foliage.

The two of us stand silently at the window for a few more minutes, staring out at the grounds. Eventually, Cecily steps back and gestures to the surrounding room.

"I hope the room is alright. I thought you might like to be on this side of the house since it's a little more private. Parker brought up your bags and put them in the closet for you," she gestures to the large double wooden doors on the other side of the room. "Take your time to unpack and get cleaned up. If you need anything, let me know, otherwise come down to the kitchen when you're ready. We can have a bite to eat and talk some more." She retrieves her book from the chair and crosses gracefully to the doorway, her pretty silver bangles jingling as she walks. "It really is nice to have you here, Stella," she says softly, stepping out of the room and closing the door behind her.

In the fading evening light, I sit back down on the edge of the bed and take in the bedroom my aunt chose for me. You could easily fit three of my apartments in this single room. Two huge windows make up most of the back wall, with the queen-sized mattress and dove gray headboard nestled between them, and the soft, subtle pattern in the duvet cover picking up the turquoise shade of the wingback chair.

The plush silvery carpet is soft and thick, and I can't help but squish it between my toes as I cross the room to the imposing closet doors. Once I get close enough, I realize the closet doors seem oddly familiar. Running my fingers over the softly burnished wood, inlaid with delicate carvings of twinkling stars and winding vines, I recognize the same beautiful craftsmanship and design from the box Cecily sent me.

Huh. So not store-bought then. I wonder who the woodworker in the family was.

Opening the oversized doors, my laughter bubbles out at the ridiculous sight of my little bag on the floor of the cavernous walk-in closet. The delicate scent of lavender is

26

stronger in here, mixed with a warm, woodsy smell I can't quite identify. My suitcase takes all of two minutes to empty; I stash most of the contents in the built-in drawers and hang the single dress I brought on one of the empty padded hangers. Grabbing my purse and backpack, I toss both on the bed and follow my nose down to the kitchen for something to eat and hopefully some answers.

Hungrier than I thought I would be, we eat dinner quietly, sitting side by side on tall bar stools at the long white kitchen island. The occasional pleasantry and light conversation about my life in New York the only communication passing between us until I sit back with a sigh.

"So." I shift to face Cecily. "What's the deal?" I ask bluntly, crumpling my napkin and dropping it beside my now empty plate.

"You certainly are a Bradleigh," Cecily laughs, turning on her stool to face me. "We tend to not deal well with the unknown, and rarely put up with anybody's shit." My eyes widen slightly at her relaxed manner. She pauses as if trying to figure out where to begin. "How much do you know about your mother's life before you were born?"

My mind tracks backward, searching for information. There are potholes in my memory big enough to swallow Volkswagens on a good day. I guess it makes some kind of fucked up sense I wouldn't remember anything about her past. Or did she just never volunteer that information? Sitting here in this place I never knew existed, with an aunt I don't know, it hits me for the first time how secretive the woman who raised me actually was.

The discomfort I feel must show on my face because

Cecily reaches out and puts her hand over mine. Jerking my hand away and pretending not to notice the flash of hurt that flits across her features, I stand and start to pace the gourmet kitchen that runs almost the entire length of the back of the house.

"Why can't I remember her ever telling me about her past? How come I don't know any stories about my grandparents? How did I not know I had an aunt until a few days ago?" My pulse starts to gallop like a runaway horse, and I can feel my face flushing. "I can tell you her favorite color, her favorite perfume, and what she liked on her burgers. I can draw you a fucking diagram of the freckles on her cheeks. But I can't tell you the name of her best friend growing up. I can't tell you where she went to school or why she ran from this place."

By this time, I'm no longer just pacing; I'm *angry* pacing. Stomping.

"What kind of fucking mother has no past? What kind of shitty daughter never thinks to ask about it? *Did* I ask about it and just can't remember? Why can't I remember?" My sentences start to bleed together in my gathering rage, giving an authentic voice to the frustration and fear that I suspect have been building in me for years. Panic, my faithful pain in the ass companion, starts to flutter her black wings. Spinning on my heel with my breathing turning shallow and rapid, I stare Cecily straight in the face.

"What the fuck is going on? Why am I here? Who the hell am I? What do you want from me?" I rudely yell at the top of my lungs. The rational part of my brain keeps telling me to shut up, but oh God, my panicked self is such an asshole. This woman has been nothing but kind to me, and here I am, screaming at her like every bad thing that's ever happened to me is her fault. Unfortunately, recognizing my

28

shitty behavior doesn't make it any easier to stop once the freak-out starts. Now she's going to hate me and send me away before I get any real answers.

Standing and walking forward slowly, likely trying to avoid spooking the psychotic-looking, wide-eyed mess in front of her any further, Cecily reaches out, grasps both of my shaking hands tightly, and simply breathes with me.

No judgment.

No accusations.

No fear.

And as she stands there, silently accepting of my flip-out, my own breathing starts to calm and my heart feels less like it's going to explode out of my chest.

How did she do that?

This woman I met only this morning has somehow instantly made me feel less alone in the world. That in itself should freak me out, but it does just the opposite.

"I'm sorry," I whisper. "For yelling at you like that, and for the other thing. On the porch earlier."

Her peal of laughter startles me.

"You think that's the first time somebody has thrown up on that porch? Or even on my shoes for that matter? Have I got stories for you, my girl." She reaches up and tucks a strand of shiny raven black hair behind my ear affectionately.

"Stella," she starts, "I can't tell you what happened in your past, or why your mom had you both using fake names, or even why she ran away from here, but I can tell you I will help you figure it out. Something horrible happened, and that's all I know. I will share whatever I can about your mother when she was young, about our family, about *your* family. We can figure this all out together." Her voice quivers with long unshed tears.

"Tweedvale is where you belong. I would like you to stay. Please stay."

Lifting my eyes to meet hers, her tension is visible, anticipating my argument to leave and go back to New York. As tempting as the idea of running back to normal is, something is telling me my path has shifted, and my normal will never be the same. There are answers I need that I can only find here, with Cecily's help. I need to find out what other secrets my mother was keeping, and why they were so important they cost us both the family we deserved. I want to learn about my aunt and explore the life that would have been mine all along.

"What about my apartment back in New York?" I ask with caution. Just thinking about having to go back to dealing with Creeper Todd and his grabby hands right now makes me throw up in my mouth a little, but I need to know I still have a place to go back to if this doesn't work out. "It's not the best set-up in the world, but it's mine. And I also have to make sure it's okay with my boss if I take some extra time off."

I start mindlessly biting my left thumbnail. Cecily smiles and reaches out to gently pull my hand away from my mouth, just like my mom used to do.

"We can keep up the rent on your apartment for now. I'm sure your landlord won't care where you are as long as he's getting his money. As for work, even from the small amount you told me about your friend Sally at dinner, it sounds like she'll understand why you want to stay here for a little while." The hope that shines from her pretty face reaches through my defenses and touches my lonely hidden heart, making my decision easier.

"Okay, I'll stay. At least for a little while."

With that one sentence, all of my mother's warnings and

my promises to her turn to dust, and unbeknownst to me, a terrifying game that had been on pause since my mother left here, starts up again.

Choking back something between a sniffle and a laugh, Cecily wraps me in a bear hug and dances us around the kitchen.

$\mathcal{A}$fter what might have been the best night's sleep I've ever had, I wander downstairs the next morning in search of something to satisfy my rumbling stomach. Admiring the beautiful art adorning the walls along the way, I'm totally not paying attention to where I'm going.

"Good morning, Miss Bradleigh." I nearly jump out of my skin as Spry rounds the corner and smoothly sidesteps just in time to avoid me crashing into him.

"Good morning!" I reply, at a higher volume than necessary, startled out of my daydreams. "Rule number one, don't gawk and walk." I scold myself out loud, and we both laugh.

"Your aunt is in the kitchen, Miss Bradleigh," he says as he moves past me on his way to the front of the house.

"Thanks, Spry. And it's just Stella!" I call to his retreating back before he closes the heavy front door behind him.

Cecily is leaning against the counter in front of a complicated-looking contraption that is chugging and wheezing and spewing out a thin stream of something that may or may not be coffee. She looks up as I walk into the kitchen, and once again, her resemblance to my mother makes my heart squeeze.

"Good morning. How did you sleep?" She gives me a cheerful smile while the machine in front of her spits the last of its dark brown liquid into her waiting cup.

"Oddly enough, I slept well, thanks. I'm usually a light sleeper, especially in new places. Kind of the whole one eye open thing." I shift nervously, not quite sure if I should sit or stand or run. I'm rusty at being anything but alone. Cecily senses my awkwardness and offers me a distraction in the form of a glass of orange juice before shooing me over to the long kitchen table. She follows close behind with her coffee and a plate of fresh muffins.

"I didn't know what you liked to eat for breakfast, so I thought this would be a safe choice before we go register you for school," she says and sits down across from me.

Miraculously, I manage not to choke to death on the chunk of blueberry muffin I just stuffed in my mouth. I chug half my juice and stare open-mouthed at her, hoping my ears misheard what she just said. Cecily stares right back, neither of us giving an inch.

"School." The word tastes like chalk in my mouth.

"School," she repeats. "Since you're going to be staying here, at least for a while, you might as well focus on your senior year and start looking at colleges. You've only missed three weeks of classes." She shrugs. "Go get ready, and we'll finish getting you registered."

College. I've never even considered college a possibility. I'm smart, yeah, and I got decent grades right up until my sophomore year in high school. When shit fell apart, school became the least of my worries, and my grades suffered. I switched from traditional high school to an online program to at least try to graduate eventually, but it's still

34

been challenging to find time for everything I need to do in a day. Besides that, there has never been a remote chance of being able to pay for college, even if my grades *were* stellar.

Once the initial shock wears off, I realize Cecily said *finish* getting me registered.

"Finish?" I question. "Oh, Auntie dear, how can we finish something we haven't even started yet?" I squint at her across the table, one eyebrow raised in suspicion. She just laughs her tinkly laugh and brushes me off with a wave.

"What can I say, I'm an optimist. As soon as you told me you were coming, I *might* have called a friend at Woodington to advise them you would be enrolling." With that little nugget of truth, she turns and floats out of the kitchen, leaving me gaping after her.

Woodington is actually Woodington Academy, an imposing century-old institution of higher learning with a storied history and a long line of fantastically successful alumni. At least that's the line the headmistress tried to spoon-feed me at the very long and very dull registration meeting yesterday.

Both Cecily and my mother were students here at one time, though only Cecily graduated. Her strong ties to the school might explain how I bypassed the substantial waiting list and was allowed to enroll after the start of the school year.

Almost like magic, my aunt had five complete uniforms appear in my closet overnight, pressed and hanging perfectly. Dark navy blazers, charcoal skirts, crisp white shirts, and a choice of long navy socks or tights. I'm even wearing a tie, for fuck's sake, though I had to ask Spry to teach me how to knot it properly.

Dressed in what feels like borrowed finery, I'm glad my shoes are still all me. One thing Cecily didn't think of was footwear, and oh boy, was she kicking herself for that this morning when she saw these beauties. My well-worn black and white Vans make me smile as I stare down at them, remembering Sally calling them my Spicoli slides. When I told her I didn't know what that meant, she made me watch Fast Times at Ridgemont High with her after calling me a heathen.

My smile falters as a perfect pair of high-heeled black patent Mary Janes step into view, rousing me from my thoughts.

Here we go.

"Stella Bradleigh?" the shoes ask politely in a lilting, smoky voice. Looking up, I'm struck by the silver-blonde beauty of the girl standing in front of me with her hand held out in greeting.

"Yeah. Hi." I stumble over my words a little. "I'm she. She's me."

Fuuuuuuck. Deep breath, spaz.

"Sorry. Hi. Yes, I'm Stella."

"I'm Sunday Easton, and I've been assigned as your peer mentor to show you around Woodington." She shakes my hand with a much firmer grip than I expected and grins down at my feet in appreciation. "Love your shoes. There's a hot pink pair of Chuck Taylors I keep hidden in the back of my closet so my mother can't find them and throw them out." Sticking her nose in the air, she says in her best haughty fake British accent, "Eastons don't wear sneakers, Sunday Grace." She rolls her warm hazel eyes and then laughs at the look of disbelief on my face at the mention of her middle name. "Oh yes, it's true, but don't worry, I do my best to *not* live up to the name. Perfect saintly Mother would shit twice and die if she knew half the things *this* Easton does." She grins and jerks her thumb at her chest for emphasis.

Something in Sunday's manner and easy laugh makes me instantly comfortable. My gut tells me I can be friends with this girl, no problem. My whole life, I've been conditioned to stand apart and keep everybody except my mother at a safe distance. Maybe it's time for something different. We spend the next few minutes comparing notes on books we've both read, movies we've seen, and music we love. Who knew a California rich girl would have tastes so in line with a poor girl from small-town New York?

The school secretary, clearly annoyed with our conversation, manages to ask us *almost* politely to take it elsewhere. I follow Sunday out through the office door, and into the crowd of students milling around in the front foyer. We've got about forty minutes before our first class, so I'm surprised to see so many kids already here. Surrounded by all the visible privilege and wealth, I'm a little off my game. So much so, that I walk right into the back of my guide as she comes to an abrupt halt in front of me.

"Shit! Sorry!" I apologize and rub my nose where it connected solidly with the back of her skull.

Get it together. What did we say yesterday? Don't gawk and walk!

Sunday turns back to me, flipping her angelic hair over her shoulder.

"Don't worry about it, New Girl. I mean, I *do* have a rather awe-inspiring ass so I can see why you'd be more interested in staring at it than paying attention to where you're walking."

For the next ten seconds, I'm not sure whether this girl is for real or not as she stands there, all straight-faced and serious-looking. At my stricken expression, she finally relents and unleashes a belly laugh that's totally at odds with her polished rich-girl exterior.

"Relax! I'm kidding! I know you're probably completely overwhelmed right now, but it's all good." She reaches out and gives my hand a quick squeeze and then points across the hall to the bank of lockers lining the wall. "That's where we are. Yours is two over from mine." She threads her way nimbly through the other students and glances back over her shoulder when she realizes I haven't moved. "Stella?" she questions. "You coming?"

"What? Oh, sorry. With that kind of lead-up, I had to check out the goods for myself." I reach up and tap my index finger against my lip thoughtfully. "I'd give it a solid seven," I say decisively as I join her at our lockers. For a split second, her face freezes in shock before she lets out another one of her belly laughs.

"Oh, hells to the no! This ass is a straight-up ten, bish!" she proudly proclaims, cocking her hip and smacking her butt cheek for emphasis.

Grinning and waggling my eyebrows at her, I lean my shoulder against the row of cold metal locker doors as she grabs what she needs for class. On the way to our shared homeroom, she points out various helpful landmarks like restrooms, the library, and the cafeteria.

As we walk, I start to covertly notice the attention Sunday draws and appears to be oblivious to. The guys here stare at her almost predatorily with undisguised lust, while the girls eye her with an odd mixture of wannabe awe and distaste. And all of them move just slightly out of her way as we pass, almost ceremoniously.

My observations are cut short, however, when Sunday grabs my wrist and detours us toward a group of students crowded around large double doors. Snippets of music and laughter float from the room within.

"This is The Aud. Home of anything remotely fun that happens at this school. This is where the auditions and rehearsals for the annual senior class Christmas gala are held." My face scrunches in confusion at her mention of Christmas since it's only the end of September, and she laughs. "Seems excessive, right? I have no idea why, but it always starts in September. Tradition, maybe?" She gives me a wink, moving inside and down the stairs to three students lounging in the plush seats a few rows back from the stage. I follow, mostly because I'm not sure what else to do.

The room is beautiful and like none I've ever been in. About thirty tiered rows, with aisles dividing them into three equal sections, rise gracefully from the elevated stage down at the front of the space. And while the seats still fold down like standard old-school movie theater seats, they're covered in a velvety deep blue material and are probably more comfortable than my bed back in New York. By the time I reach Sunday and her group, I am once again sure this must be a dream or a mistake. There is no way somebody like me would be allowed into a place like this.

"Stella, meet Aylie, Payne, and Roxy. Guys, this is Stella Bradleigh." Sunday pats the empty seat next to her, and I flop into it gratefully. I'm saved from having to do anything more than return the friendly smiles of the girls and the nod from the lone guy in the group by the opening cowbell from Marvin Gaye's 'Got To Give It Up' booming through The Aud's impressive sound system. A loud collective cheer erupts from the students in the room, none more piercing than the high-pitched screeching generated by three girls standing together in the front row. Leaning over to Sunday, I yell so she can hear me over the racket.

"If those girls throw their panties on stage, I am so out of here," I threaten with a laugh.

"Don't joke!" she laughs back. "I'm pretty sure they've tried to do more than throw their panties at them." With that somewhat gross visual, she stands, gives a small salute to the group we are sitting with, and motions for me to follow her through the row to the far exit aisle. The music is loud and infectious, and I find myself bobbing my head and sort of dancing along behind her.

When we get to the stairs, I can see the stage clearly, so I grab her sleeve, wanting to stop and watch. Three guys are on stage, conga-lining like idiots and singing along to the music. Too foolish to be part of a Christmas gala, it looks more like a highly successful attempt to annoy the plain-looking girl also on stage trying in vain to call the next person up to audition.

Sunday is dancing beside me, and I forget myself long enough for us to give each other a few disco-flavored hip bumps as we laugh and cheer along with the crowd.

Even in a group of rowdy teenagers, my new friend stands out, and the guys on stage catch sight of us. Two of them send her huge grins and thumbs ups in approval. The third, though, he looks straight at me, winds his hips, and winks audaciously. Caught up in the music and the moment, I throw my head back and fully laugh for the first time in what feels like forever. My laughter turns to ash in my throat when I look back at the stage. Now openly staring at me, recognition slides over his striking features and sinks into my gut.

You've got to be fucking kidding me.

Suddenly extremely uncomfortable, I whirl around and

take off up the stairs to the exit, my face flushed, and my heart racing.

Once back in the hallway, I run straight for the restrooms we passed earlier. Finding an open stall at the far end, I slam the door behind me, locking it and resting my forehead against the dark wood. Squeezing my eyes shut, I silently will myself to disappear. A few minutes pass, my short, sharp breaths the only sounds in the cavernous room before the main door bangs open.

"New Girl? Are you in here?" Footsteps make their way down the row of stalls, stopping at each door and testing the lock on it until she finally gets to mine. I open my eyes and see the toes of her shoes peeking under the door. Hiding from her at this point is useless, and ignoring her would be incredibly rude, so I step back and flip the lock, allowing the door to swing inward and reveal me in all my freaked-out glory. "What the hell happened back there?" Sunday's face and voice exhibit nothing but worry.

"I, uh, suffer from a bit of a panic disorder, so sometimes I freak out in big groups." It's not a total lie; it just isn't the whole truth. Shrugging one shoulder and hoping she'll accept my explanation at face value, I move to make my way past her to the nearest sink. Before I can take more than two steps, her arms wrap around me in a tight hug. Pulling back, but not fully letting go, she stares me straight in the face.

"You can always tell me what's going on. You need to leave, we leave together. Just grab me and pull. For reals. You aren't alone here, Stell." The sincerity of her words and the ferocity of her hug stuns me into silence. Finding my voice again, I clear my throat and ask the obvious question.

"What's in this for you, Sunday? Why do you give a shit? You don't even know me." The words come out more bitchy than intended, but that doesn't seem to faze her.

"I knew you the minute we met, silly!" She grins like a fool at me, all perfect teeth and shiny pink lip gloss. "Kindred spirits and all that. Felt it in my gut, and the Easton gut never lies." She sticks her belly out and pats it a few times for emphasis.

"You're crazy. You know that, right?" I ask, shaking my head and grinning back.

"Oh probably, but if I am, it's the best kind of crazy!" she promises with a Girl Scout salute.

"Were you ever actually a Girl Scout?" I question with a healthy amount of skepticism.

"Not a fucking chance!" she chortles gleefully. With that not so surprising revelation, she drags me out of the restroom and down the hall to homeroom.

CHAPTER FIVE

*S*itting through my first class is torture. It's been so long since I've been in an actual classroom setting that it feels claustrophobic. Being the new girl isn't helping matters either. Usually, I'm reasonably good at tuning out what other people are doing and don't give a shit what anybody thinks of me.

Not today.

Today, these offspring of the high and mighty are making me feel like a discount sweater at a fire sale—something to be examined and then rejected for not meeting their distorted standards. One group of girls, specifically, seem particularly venomous; the poison in their eyes aimed squarely in my direction. They look vaguely familiar, but there have been so many new faces today, I could be imagining it.

"Sunday," I whisper loudly and lean over to her desk beside mine. "What's with the Bitches of Eastwick over there?" Lowering my head to hide my face from the other students around us, I flick my eyes in the direction of the three very well-accessorized and good-looking girls. Doing a miserable job stifling her hoot of laughter, she knows exactly who I'm talking about without having to look.

"That would be Hali, Laina, and Carrisa. And that is the best description for that gaggle of nasty females I've ever heard. Hali is the ringleader, and the other two are her agents of chaos." Sunday sits up straight and smiles innocently at our homeroom teacher as he shoots us the universally known face for *'shut the hell up in my classroom'*. As soon as he goes back to reading over his notes, I lean over to her again.

"Well, what the hell did I do to deserve the death glares they're shooting at me? I've been here for all of three and a half damn minutes!" I huff. I never huff. I never care enough to huff.

This place is already doing weird things to me.

"You, my dear New Girl, committed the cardinal sin," she sing-songs quietly. With that, she mimes zipping her lips and leaves me staring at her, *my* lips pressed together in frustration. Before I can demand she explain her cryptic bullshit comment, the bell rings, and we get up and roll out of the classroom in the wave of students. "Stella, I have to run to the drama room for two minutes. We both have the next period free, so go and grab a spot outside in the courtyard. I'll come find you as soon as I'm done." She steers me in the direction of the doors leading outside and waves as she strides off down the hall.

Heading outside into the warm September air, I find an empty bench under a sprawling oak. Pulling my phone and earbuds out of my bag, I sit back and indulge in some people watching with Maynard James Keenan's voice singing to me about tiny monsters. Sadly, not two minutes of peace go by before I spot three angry, haughty girls marching toward me. At least as much as anybody can march in three-inch heels, anyway.

Since I can be what you might call a contrary sort of person if you're polite, or a shit-disturber if you're not, I decide to leave my earbuds in and simply cock my head to the side, watching them with a calculated expression of vague disinterest as they approach me. The leader of this little posse, the one Sunday called Hali earlier, plants her hands on her hips and stares me down. Resigning myself to having this conversation, I sigh and pull my earbuds out of my ears.

"Can I help you?" I ask dryly without standing.

"Don't you get snotty with me, you trashy bitch," she hisses back at me. "Who do you think you are? There are rules here, and low-class sluts like you follow them, or else."

Snotty? Me?

Momentarily taken aback by her hostility, it takes me a few beats to register the rest of her words. Trashy bitch, I can handle. Low-class, well, she's not entirely wrong. But slut?

Nuh-uh. No way, no day.

I stand, pulling myself up to my full five feet and eight inches, and get nose-to-nose with Fascist Barbie.

"Look, princess, I'm sitting over here, minding my own business. What the fuck have I done to offend your delicate sensibilities? Nothing. You don't fucking know me. So. You. Don't. Get. To. Call. Me. A. Slut." I fire each staccato word at her. Though I'm genuinely bewildered by this girl's unmistakable hatred toward me, I am also seriously pissed off by her shitty attitude. "Back the fuck up, Barbie, and leave me alone. Shoo." Flicking my fingers at her dismissively, I stand my ground, waiting for her and her minions to leave. To my surprise, she leans in even closer, her cloyingly sweet perfume wrapping around me like a candy-scented lasso.

"That's not how it works here. You don't get to just show up out of the blue and jump the line." She peers spitefully down her clearly after-market nose at me. "There are rules, and just because you're a Bradleigh, don't think they don't apply to you."

Because I'm a Bradleigh? What the shit does that mean?

"You know," I tell her, "shrieking like a toddler having a tantrum is super unbecoming. Is this a rich girl thing? Do you need a time-out?" Her jaw muscles bulge right along with her eyes, and her hands ball into fists at her sides. "Seriously, if I had even a remote understanding of what the fuck you are freaking out about, I might be more concerned." I lean back slightly and give her a thoughtful once over. "Wait, no, that's a lie." I shrug. "There is no situation in which I would give a rat's ass about anything you have to say."

With that, I turn and grab my bag from the bench behind me and attempt to shove by her. Once again, I underestimate the size of her ego, and her pampered hand clamps onto my wrist, grinding the bones together painfully and stopping me short.

Damn! The girl has one hell of a grip.

I'm seconds away from breaking every one of her fingers digging into my arm, starting with the one flashing the huge emerald and rose gold ring when Sunday's voice cuts through the thunderclouds of anger and pain gathering in my brain.

"Oh, Hali, you silly girl," she clucks her tongue in mocking reproach as she sashays toward us. "You should know better than to grab people who could snap you like a toothpick." She smiles innocently. "Be a good girl and let go of Stella before she punches you in the face. I'm sure your daddy doesn't want to pay for another new nose." Sunday's soft drawl sounds somewhere between lazy and bored, but the fierce glint in her hazel eyes and the set of her jaw tells me she's anything but.

Wrenching out of Hali's grasp, I spin to face her full-on. Clear-headed enough to realize a physical altercation on my first day would probably be a bad idea, I decide to settle for a simple verbal evisceration. I open my mouth, but before a word comes out, her attention focuses on something behind me. Her previously pinched expression instantly morphs into a soft, doe-eyed mask. From my experience, there's only one thing that can make a person go from zero to Stepford that fast.

Gross. Fucking predictable females giving the rest of us a bad name.

Recognizing that anything I say to the basic bitch now will fall on deaf ears, I grit my teeth and start to walk away. Sunday isn't going to let this go that easily though and rolls her eyes in disgust at the blatant display of desperate adoration, unable to resist a parting shot.

"Jeez, have some self-respect, Hali. Drool, much?" She sneers loudly with disdain. "You might as well get down on your knees and open your mouth right here. Maybe you'll get lucky, and Poe will finally drop his pants for you."

I don't know if the group of guys I notice lounging near the doors to the school heard her, but Hali sure did. Her lips stay frozen in their pretty smile, but the rage flaring in her baby blues promises this isn't over. Not by a long shot.

Sunday and I share most of the same classes, but the last one of the day is mine alone.

"No triple threat here, missy. I sound like a basset hound being sawed in two when I sing, and I trip over my two left feet on the daily. But, boy, can I act." She sticks her head inside the music room and waggles her fingers in greeting at the teacher, grinning at his slightly nervous expression when he sees her. "He actually thanked me when I chose drama for last period this year instead of music." Blowing me an air kiss as she turns down the hall, I shake my head and laugh.

Mr. Shartun, the balding, bearded music teacher, might be my favorite so far, based solely on his sheer excitement for the subject he teaches. When I walk into his nearly empty classroom, he starts talking to me right away. He quickly explains the class is small to begin with, and a number of his students are off using the time to audition for the annual senior gala.

Honestly, after the appearance of my airport stranger on stage in The Aud this morning, and the scene with Hali the Hellion in the courtyard, the lack of bodies present right now is more than welcome.

When the final bell thankfully signals the end of the school day, I heave a sigh of relief, happy to make my way back to my locker where I spot Sunday waiting for me.

"Girl, you survived your first day!" She giggles and gives me a one-armed side squish, then turns and starts walking backward down the hall toward the main doors. "Do you need a ride home?"

"I'm good. Spry's picking me up." I had told Sunday the very bare-bones version of my story over lunch, including Cecily's driver's new nickname. "Thanks for the offer, though." Slamming my locker shut, I groan at the weight as I hoist my textbook-filled bag over my shoulder and start walking in her direction.

"No worries at all. Tell him he doesn't have to drive you tomorrow. I can pick you up and drop you off after class." I'm about to tell her she doesn't need to go out of her way for me when Sunday's grin widens as she stares down the almost empty hall over my shoulder.

My feet turn to cement, and a fluttering warmth stirs in my belly. A glance down at my arms shows me all the little hairs standing at attention.

Sandalwood and sunshine.

The soft scent winds around me like a whisper and I take a slow, deep breath. An arm brushes mine as the three guys from the stage walk by, laughing and shoving each other on their way outside.

The tallest of the three, the random hottie from the airport, looks back at me with a knowing smirk as he passes. Almost like he can tell exactly which gutter my dirty little mind dives into at the sight of him. The air crackles with the electricity between us as violet eyes clash with deep blue. He boldly holds my gaze for a few seconds longer before turning back to his friends. Rejoining their laughter, he claps the guy beside him on the back, his tattoo twining up his right arm like a living thing. All three of them offer Sunday a respectful chin lift and big grins as they pass her. The doors slam shut behind them as they leave the building, and the sound echoes around us.

"Wow. Wait. What? Did I miss something?" Sputtering and shaking her head in awe, Sunday stares at me with a grin to rival the Cheshire Cat's.

Shit. Fuck. Shitfuck.

"So, uh, yeah." I try to play it cool. "Do you happen to

know that guy's name? The tall one?" I grit my teeth, willing the heat in my lower belly to dissipate.

"Oh, *'the tall one'*, huh?" She says with air quotes and a snicker. "That, my shiny new friend, was your cardinal sin." Quickly she closes the distance between us, loops her arm through mine, and practically skips us outside. "The one and only Poe Halliday. Rich, enigmatic, and sexy as hell." She slips on her pink tortoiseshell Maui Jim's as we step into the late afternoon sunshine. "Also, the object of Hali's lust, which is why when he winked at you this morning, you became numero uno on her hit list, you bad girl." She wags her finger playfully at me, then shrugs. "He hasn't so much as sneezed in her direction in three years, but that hasn't dampened the torch she carries for him. Poe and his boys rule the school and the town."

"Well, that's fucking fantastic, isn't it?" I mutter. "I've been here one day, and I'm already the target of the Queen Bitch." Spotting the Caddy with Spry behind the wheel, I give Sunday a tired smile and pull my arm free, telling her I'll see her tomorrow and escaping before she has a chance to comment further. The cocoon of the car's backseat a welcome retreat, I gratefully sink into the luxurious comfort with a sigh.

"Rough first day, Stella?" Spry's sympathetic eyes meet mine as he glances over his shoulder.

"I'm pretty sure I have no idea what I've gotten myself into, Spry." Breaking contact, I close my eyes, jam my earbuds in, and lose myself in the music.

CHAPTER SIX

POE

*W*hen I see her dancing on the aisle stairs, her glossy raven hair a stark contrast against Sunday's silvery blonde, I shoot her a sly wink and wonder who she is and how long it'll take me to get into her pants.

It's not until she throws her head back and laughs with abandon that my blood sings with recognition, and I almost trip over Heller in my surprise. My recovery is quick, but I can tell, at least for a brief minute, my shock is written clearly on my face. I see the same expression mirrored on her beautiful features, followed by a slight blush of embarrassment, and she runs.

Good. She should run from me. Fast and far enough that I can't catch her.

I can't help my cocky grin when I think about just how much fun catching her would be, though. The memory of my hand wrapped up in that gorgeous, thick, dark hair makes me instantly hard. Groaning internally, I'm glad my white button-down is untucked and offers at least a little coverage.

Down, boy.

I force my focus back to the bit of fun two of my boys and I are having, continuing in our attempt to annoy the mouse of a stagehand. That's part of being us—we get away with acting like the entitled, arrogant asses most people think we are. Nobody here would dare question anything my three best friends and I do, so we practically have free rein, which means we do things like this sometimes to remind ourselves that we're still breathing.

Payne, Heller, Raff, and I have been best friends pretty much since birth. Our families have lived in this exclusive little town since forever and are viewed as pillars of the community. For the most part, on the outside, we look exactly like what we're supposed to be—the well-bred first-born sons of the wealthiest and most powerful families in the state. On the inside, we're anything but. Not one of us wants to follow the paths our families have laid out for us, and not one of us genuinely believes we have any means of escape. We know the day will come, not too far from now, when each of us is forced to conform to the expectations of our lineage and our lives will no longer be our own. We will be forced to marry the women, work the jobs, and father the children our parents dictate.

So, to pass the time and feel like we have some semblance of control, we are the bad boys of Folkestone. Some of us prefer ink, and some of us metal; I crave the fleeting pain of both. We drive too fast, drink too much, fuck whoever we want, and continually wish for a way out. Raff almost succeeded last year, though not in the way he hoped, when he rolled his Porsche Cayman GT4 down an embankment and totaled it. He spent four weeks in the hospital and has a jagged scar across his ribs that girls seem to love.

One of us was with him every day of those four weeks.

His parents were there twice.

I gave up the idea that this life was something I wanted long ago, but I also thought I gave up on the idea of being able to leave it behind. Then a chance run-in with a beautiful dark-haired stranger who rose to my unspoken challenge showed me a brief glimpse of the other side; what it was like to feel alive. Of course, being interrupted by my mother was a mood killer. When my phone rang, I wanted nothing more than to drop it to the ground and crush it under my heel. I felt physical pain as the stranger pulled her strong, feminine body away from mine and smiled at me with that sexy mouth.

Just thinking about the silky feel of her lips is making my boxer briefs uncomfortably tight again.

Fucking hell.

The memory of her hasn't faded since that afternoon at the airport, and that pisses me off. Seeing her here now pisses me off even more. I don't get attached. Ever. The only reason to fuck a girl is to get off, and then they cease to exist in my world. Don't get me wrong, angry or not, I *will* finish what we started and get her out of my system. I don't have to like her to fuck her, and when I've had my fill of those lush curves, I'll drop her just like all the others.

The fourth in our little circle, Payne, is down in the third row with Roxy and Aylie, so after we jokingly take our bows, we jump down and join them. My oldest friend sees something of interest in my expression and looks at me questioningly. Scowling back at him, he lets it go, his hands up in mock surrender. He knows I'll talk when I'm good and ready.

I'm trying like hell to come up with a nonchalant way to ask the girls if they know who Sunday's with, but before I get the chance, the pit viper known as Hali Torsten slithers her way over to our little group, swaying her hips provocatively.

"Poe, that was just amazing," she breathes, staring up at me all doe-eyed. "You're so funny!" She giggles, the sound instantly grating on my last nerve.

Don't get me wrong, it's not that she's not a good-looking girl; most guys would probably give their left nut to have her look at them the way she looks at me. But I'm not most guys. I know precisely what drives Hali, and the twisted vein of malice and hate that runs through her. There is no way I would ever have anything to do with her, though our parents seem to have other plans.

Shaking her unwelcome touch off my arm, I nod slightly toward the exit. Taking my cue, Payne and Heller lead the way, then me, with Raff, Roxy, and Aylie bringing up the rear. The warning sound Hali makes as we walk away isn't lost on me.

That's going to bite me in the ass later.

Once out in the hallway, our group splits up as we all head off to our respective classes. Since Payne and I share the next period, we walk together in silence for a few minutes.

"So. You know who Sunday was with earlier?"

"Who? The dark-haired hottie?" Payne asks with a sly grin. He knows me way too well to fall for my shitty attempt at being casual. "That would be Stella Bradleigh." I suck in a breath.

Bradleigh? The Bradleigh Heir is back in town? If that's true, my mother is going to lose her mind.

"Why, you interested, Halliday?"

"As more than a toy? Never. Looks like she might be fun for a night or two, though." I shrug it off as we enter the classroom and slide into our seats.

54

"Sure," he draws out the word like it's the stupidest thing he's ever heard. "If you say so, bro." Payne laughs and shakes his head.

Aiming my best glare in his direction only makes him laugh harder, so I spend the rest of the class ignoring his dumb ass instead.

Every year, tradition dictates that the entire senior class has the second period free, and it's usually spent catching up on homework, sleep, or gossip.

From our alcove in the courtyard, I spot her under a tree on the other side of the green space. Watching her while she watches everybody else intrigues me, and the conversation around me fades into the background.

Calm and quiet, she still commands attention, a strange combination of badass and soft uncertainty. Almost like she's been kicked in the gut one too many times and isn't a hundred percent sure she can get up again, but sure as hell is going to try.

The rapid tapping of angry high heels on cement pierces through the fog of my musings like gunfire, and I catch movement from the corner of my eye.

Shit. Hali. I wonder if she knows?

She doesn't pay me any attention as she leads her hand-maidens of mayhem straight to Stella. Payne notices too and nudges me with his foot.

"Think we should do something about that?" he asks, his voice low.

"Let it play out. What is she to us anyway?" I can feel Payne's disapproving stare as I lean my head back against the wall, feigning disinterest.

Curious to see how she handles herself, I watch covertly while the conversation of my friends continue to swirl around me. I'm too far away to hear what's being said between the girls, but if body language is any indicator, it isn't good. Stella stands, her back ramrod straight and her face stony, getting right in her adversary's face.

Good for you, Bradleigh. You're going to need that attitude here.

Her little dismissive finger flick makes me chuckle quietly, and I glance away quickly as Payne and Heller both turn at the sound.

When I look back, the scene has moved closer. It looks like Stella may have tried to walk away and now has her wrist caught in an overly manicured death grip. Even from here, I can almost hear the bones grinding painfully together and wonder what sort of mark that's going to leave on her porcelain flesh.

"Fuck, dude, she's one of us. We can't just let Hali rough her up like that." Payne's voice is quiet but stern.

"We don't know what she is to us yet, and I'll wager neither does she." My tone makes it clear the matter isn't open for discussion, but Payne, choosing to ignore me, moves to stand just as Sunday arrives on the scene. Lowering himself back down, the two of us watch the drama unfold.

Whatever the silvery blonde adds to the already volatile mix has to be *really* unflattering. Hali looks like she would happily set both Sunday *and* Stella on fire at this point, and that makes me laugh for real this time. The sound must carry through the breeze because Hali looks over, noticing that both Payne and I are watching. The way her expression changes like melting wax disgusts me.

Such a fake-ass bitch.

The distraction allows Stella to pull her arm free when she realizes the focus is no longer on her. Shaking her head in disgust, she starts to walk away, but Sunday, being Sunday, can't just let it slide. She hooks her arm through Stella's, and whatever parting shot she lobs at Hali has the nasty bitch trying her hardest to hold on to her vapid smile while her eyes betray the barely contained rage directed at the two girls in front of her. Dark and light head back into the school arm in arm, and the guys and I close ranks and follow shortly after.

Heller and Raff are waiting for me at the end of the day. The two of them leaning nonchalantly against the bank of lockers is causing the usual array of admiring feminine smiles and giggles. Heller ignores it for the most part, but Raff, always the flirt, eats it up.

"Bro, why do you encourage them?" Heller punches him in the arm.

"Why not?" Raff winks at a group of girls walking by, setting them all off tittering like a flock of little birds. "*I* know they don't have a chance, and *you* know they don't have a chance, but *they* don't need to know that."

"Rafferty Essex, giving hope to desperate girls every-where." I punch him in his other arm as I join them, and the three of us laugh as he takes an elaborate bow in the middle of the hallway.

I dump my books in my locker and moving as a single unit, we make our way through the school. As we start down the hall that leads toward the exit doors, I'm greeted by the sight of long dark hair spilling halfway down to a luscious ass, and legs for miles, somehow made even sexier

57

in the over-the-knee socks some of the girls choose to wear instead of tights. Never has a pair of socks looked so damn hot. Once again, my dick swells at the sight of her.

For fuck's sake, why does she have this effect on me?

Sunday, who is walking backward down the hall, sees us coming and smiles knowingly, her eyes flicking between Stella and I. Stella herself appears to be glued to the spot where she stands. I can almost hear the magnetic hum between us as the guys and I approach from behind.

When we get close enough, I make sure my arm brushes against hers on my way past, and I can't stop myself from turning and looking over my shoulder to see her reaction. I feel the challenge rise in my eyes again, and again hers spark back at me in response. The pull between us is undeniable, and I wouldn't stop the jackass smirk that lifts the corner of my mouth even if I could.

Focusing again on my friends, I clap Raff on the back, and we shove through the doors into the lot. Telling the guys I'd talk to them later, I slide behind the wheel of my Vantage AMR and take a few minutes to adjust myself, figuratively and literally. Leaning my head back against the red leather headrest, I pound the steering wheel a few times with the flat of my palm.

Why am I letting this girl get under my skin?

She may be hanging out with the crowd a Bradleigh would be expected to, but I don't think that's why she's doing it. I'm pretty sure she doesn't know what being a Bradleigh Heir even means, or how my being a Halliday affects her.

And I'm positive she has no idea what she's gotten herself into.

CHAPTER SEVEN

STELLA

My dreams are filled with shrieking shadows and a dark fog of memories, stitched together by sharp teeth and jagged nails. Waking, sweaty and agitated, to the sound of my frantic breathing, I grab my phone from the charging dock on my nightstand and wince when the screen shows me it's only 4:17 a.m. Weighing my options, I decide to get up and shower, thinking maybe I can get a head start on some of my homework. I've only missed the first three and a half weeks of classes, but the curriculum at Woodington is more demanding than the online courses I had been taking back in New York, so I still have a lot of catching up to do.

My aunt finds me two and a half hours later, camped out at the kitchen table, furiously scribbling in a spiral-bound notebook while munching on a piece of peanut butter toast. I have to give it to her; she didn't pry when I got home from school yesterday, choosing instead to accept my flat two-or-three-word answers when she asked how my day had been. Immediately after dinner, I pleaded exhaustion and went to my room, where I read and listened to music until I fell into my horror show of fitful and disturbing dreams.

Somehow, the look on her face this morning tells me the matched set of baggage I'm carrying under my eyes is going to make it much harder to avoid in-depth questions this time. Just as I brace myself for the inevitable, the door chimes go off, and I'm saved by Spry ushering Sunday into the room, looking entirely too cheerful for this early on a school day.

"Morning, New Girl." Reaching across the table, she grabs the half-eaten toast out of my hand and finishes it. "Morning, Miss B."

Sure, Sunday, you can finish my breakfast.

I sigh dramatically.

"I don't suppose you're going to stop calling me New Girl anytime soon, are you?"

"Nope." She shakes her head with a big cheerful grin on her face, popping the P emphatically.

"You two know each other?" I ask grumpily, rolling my shoulders to try to ease some of the tension, either from my shitty sleep or being hunched over my homework.

"Everybody knows Miss B, Stella. She's famous around here." I swivel my head toward my aunt, surprise widening my eyes. Cecily snorts out a laugh.

"That's reaching a little." Shaking her head wryly, she hands my far too chipper friend a napkin to wipe the crumbs from her lips. "I think infamous might be closer to the truth."

While I am now super curious about *that* statement, exploring it further will have to wait until I feel less like a crusty, sleep-deprived asshole. Cecily and Sunday chat with each other about the locals I've never heard of while I haphazardly shove my books into my bag. Grabbing my friend by the arm, I lead her forcefully from the room mid-sentence, yelling goodbye to my aunt and leaving her staring after us in surprise at our hasty exit.

"In a rush to get to school or something?" Sunday asks, laughing at my scowl.

"Just didn't feel like answering questions about how my first day was," I grumble.

The entire ride to school is filled with angry chick rock blaring from the silver Range Rover's upgraded speakers. Once Sunday parks in the student lot at school, though, she shuts off the ignition, and there's no more noise from the car stereo to fill the silence between us.

She turns to face me and leans back against her door, crossing her arms and waiting for me to say something. I know she's looking for an explanation for what happened yesterday after The Aud and later with Poe in the hallway. Fidgeting with the hem of my skirt, my knees become the most fascinating thing ever. For the next thirty seconds, I stare at them intently while silently begging for her to just leave it alone. Sneaking a peek from the corner of my eye, I can see she's not giving in and is still sitting there, watching me with an exasperated expression and giving no indication that she plans to vacate the SUV anytime soon.

"Fine," I yell, "have it your way! Ask your damn questions." I pout in frustration. Dropping the edge of my skirt, I turn and flop my back against the passenger door like a three-year-old being told no. Narrowing my eyes, I wait for the inquisition to start.

By the time the question period is over, she's going to think I'm some damaged slutty nut job who isn't worth her time. We might as well get this over with now before either of us invests any more time into our friendship.

"What are you afraid of?" she asks bluntly, not breaking

eye contact with me. "At first I thought you running off from The Aud yesterday was just first-day jitters, but now I don't think it is. You flinch a little whenever somebody comes up behind you. You avoid even basic questions about your past. I know you're afraid of something. And what the hell was that in the hall with Poe?"

A harsh laugh bubbles out of me, unexpected and awkward, causing her to startle in surprise. Shaking my head slightly and blowing out a loud sigh, I fight against my natural tendency to deflect and make the conscious choice to be honest with her.

"I don't know what I'm scared of." Those words deepen the furrows on her forehead like she thinks I'm full of shit. "No, really, I don't know," I explain. "There are a couple of obvious things that add to my anxiety, of course. I mean, hello, California and magically appearing family." I pause. "Beyond that, though, I have some pretty huge memory holes, and when I look over the edge of them, things get black and scary. It forces me to step back before whatever lives inside swallows me whole."

Running my hand through the loose ebony waves falling over my shoulder, I watch the strands slide through my fingers rather than look at Sunday. Heaving a deep breath, I pull my water bottle out of my bag and take a few big swallows. This next part was going to suck hard, and the words feel thick in my throat.

Just get through this. She wouldn't be sitting here listening to your sob story if she didn't care.

"I got beat up badly a few times in the group home I lived in after my mom disappeared. Like, really badly. Fighting back would have just landed me somewhere even worse, so I ran." Her eyes widen slightly. "Things on my own got dicey a few times, and some bad shit went down,

62

but I learned how to fight when it was necessary and discovered I'm way more resilient than I ever thought." Shrugging dismissively, I keep my eyes downcast. "I took care of myself and was on my own for two years before Aunt Cecily somehow found me. Swooped in like a fairy godmother and asked me to come to California by sending me a letter in a wooden box."

Finally daring to look up at my friend, I'm shocked to see silent tears painting mucky mascara trails down her cheeks. I glance back at my hands, now twisting nervously together in my lap, and force myself to continue.

"I wasn't lying to you yesterday about having a panic disorder. Music has always helped me deal with the anxiety, but over the past year or so, I discovered something else that works really well too." The next sentence comes out in a whoosh, all the words stuck together in one big breath. "Sex works really well at quieting my brain and letting me escape for a little while, and it's probably not the best solution, but sometimes it was all I had. It's not like I was out sleeping with anybody who asked; I've only ever had two boyfriends, and it was only with them. I can't believe I told you all that."

I suck in a breath.

And another one.

"As far as Poe goes," I smile ruefully, "let's just say we had an interesting meet and greet at the airport when my plane landed." I look up to see curiosity briefly cross her features, followed by resolve as she reaches her hand out for one of mine. Gripping tight before she speaks, she chooses her words carefully.

"Thank you," she begins earnestly, "for trusting me enough to share with me. I'll always keep your secrets, and if you decide you want to explore any of those memory holes, I'll be standing at the edge beside you, with a miner's hat and a boxed lunch."

Staring at each other across the SUV's interior, we take in each other's tears and runny eye makeup. We both start laughing hysterically for no apparent reason, and the oppressive atmosphere in the car fades along with a small bit of the weight I've been carrying solo for so long.

Stopping in the nearest restroom, we fix our makeup and make it to homeroom with half a minute to spare. We sit through the monotonous morning announcements before the first-period bell goes, and Mr. Morris, our gnome-like homeroom teacher, releases us all to head to class.

On the way to English, Sunday keeps up a brutally sarcastic commentary of her uptight mother's latest quest for eternal youth. Apparently, in Mrs. Easton's eyes, it wasn't cleanliness that was next to godliness, it was youth-fulness. And she spares no expense in her attempt to fight her advancing age. Only about half of what Sunday is saying registers with my distracted brain, though. The skin on the back of my neck keeps tingling with the weight of a hallway full of stares, but every time I casually glance around, nobody seems to be looking in our direction. Chalking it up to an overactive imagination, I try to tune back into Sunday's monologue, and manage to smile and insert enough non-committal noises to pass for paying attention.

The rest of the morning plays out much the same way; Sunday keeps up a steady stream of chatter in between classes, while I keep feeling like people are staring at me and whispering behind their hands. Finally, the bell signaling our lunch period chimes. Everything about Woodington drips money and privilege, and the food is no exception.

"Seriously, this pasta bar is my new best friend," I declare blissfully. Sunday nods vigorously in absolute agreement as we fill our plates with porcini mushroom and prosciutto lasagna and sides of Caesar salad. I have no idea what a porcini mushroom even is, but the lasagna smells like heaven. As we leave the line with trays in hand, we see Aylie and Roxy waving at us from a large table near the windows and make our way over to join them.

"Ladies! Have you come to grace us with your presence today? Or merely to eat your weight in pasta?" a masculine voice teases from behind us as we sit down. Sunday jabs Payne in the ribs with her fork as he sits down beside her, laughing.

"Are you calling me fat, you buffoon?" she asks him with a look of exaggerated indignation.

"Never. Those carbs keep your ass nicely rounded, so you just keep doing what you're doing." Payne ducks just in time to avoid the dressing-covered crouton she chucks playfully at his head.

My eyes focused on my lunch, I can't keep the little smile from my lips as I listen to the two of them banter back and forth. She hasn't come out and said it to me in so many words, but I can tell Sunday has a thing for Payne. I make a mental note to ask her what's up with that situation the next time we're alone. I'm so engrossed in their little barbs and my incredibly tasty lunch that I startle when a body sits down next to me. That damn addictive scent wraps around me again. I look up, expecting to see deep blue, but I'm surprised by bright green eyes twinkling at me instead, and I'm nearly blinded by the wide grin that comes with them.

"Hiya, New Girl," he says, holding out his hand for me to

shake. When I reach for it, he flips my hand over and brings my knuckles to his lips for a quick kiss. Poe sits down across the table from me with another of the guys from The Aud yesterday and shoots a dark glare at Green Eyes. He drops my hand, laughing as Sunday pipes up with introductions.

"Mr. Smooth over there is Raff, blondie across the table is Heller, and well, I think you know who Poe is." She coughs delicately to cover her grin. "Guys, this is Stella. Play nice. The girls and I like her and don't want you chasing her off." Roxy and Aylie both nod in agreement.

Raff and Heller are polar opposites in looks, the former being all light eyes and shiny, nearly black hair, and the latter having blond hair almost as pale as Sunday's and eyes like dark chocolate. Both guys offer me flirty grins in greeting and then promptly dismiss me as they start debating the merits of Porsche over BMW.

Poe, however, is a whole other story. He doesn't say hi, doesn't even acknowledge I exist. He just eats his lunch, making a show of ignoring me, and occasionally interjects comments into Raff and Heller's conversation.

Alright, assclown. You want to pretend it never happened, I can too.

I spend the next twenty minutes laughing and joking with the girls and Payne when Roxy smacks herself in the forehead.

"Duh, I almost forgot! My parents have decided to stay in Paris for another week, so party at my place on Saturday." She grins. "Stella, you'll come too, right?" Feeling like a night to hang out and get to know my new friends better might be just what I need, I agree but nearly regret it when Sunday all but begs me to go shopping with her beforehand. Having a friend who is so overtly girlie is utterly new to me.

The conversation all around us suddenly quiets, and I feel the focus in the room shift to our table.

"Did I hear you're having a party, Roxy?" Hali steps up behind me, her fake-sweet tone barely disguising the chill underneath. Roxy flushes and presses her lips together, making me want to cuff Hali upside the head. Poe notices Roxy's obvious discomfort too and interjects.

"You're not invited, Hal. Maybe next time." He pauses and thoughtfully chews a bite of his lunch. "But probably not."

Sunday lets a loud snort escape before Payne jokingly clamps his hand over her mouth. He smiles innocently at Hali.

"Allergies," Payne explains to her, straight-faced as the rest of us try to stifle our laughter.

Tossing her hair in a huff, she stalks off to her table, and the cafeteria starts buzzing again.

"You guys don't think she'll actually show up, do you?" Aylie frets, her forehead furrowed. "She's so nasty. Nobody wants her around, but after what she did to…" She trails off and is quiet for a few seconds. "Well, everybody is a little afraid of her. Everybody except Poe and Sunday, that is."

"And Stella," Sunday adds with her mouth full of salad. "She went toe to toe with Hali and her merry band of bitches in the courtyard yesterday." The entire table turns to look at me with surprise.

"New Girl has some balls, does she?" Heller teases from across the table.

"Bigger than yours, pretty boy." I fire back to a chorus of laughter. An appreciative grin flits across Poe's beautiful mouth before he notices me looking and arranges his face back into the arrogant mask I'm becoming used to seeing. Heller gets up and comes around the table, pulling me up from my seat. He bear hugs me and lifts me right off my feet.

"I like New Girl, too. I say we keep her." Planting a loud kiss on my cheek, he sets me back down with a wink. Payne, Raff, and Poe all get up and join Heller, making their way toward the cafeteria exit. I wait for the girls to gather their things, and we follow the guys out, making plans for the party this weekend.

"Shit! Hang on, guys! I left my phone on the table. Be right back!" I sprint into the cafeteria and see my phone still sitting on our table across the room. Crossing quickly to grab it, I notice the odd silence descend again, and I just know Hali is behind me before I even turn around.

CHAPTER EIGHT

"We have unfinished business, you and I," Hali hisses through clenched teeth and a fake smile. "You don't belong here, and you know it. By the time I'm done, you'll regret the day you ever stepped foot in this town, and you'll be begging to crawl back to your shithole in New York." The threat hanging in the air between us, I force my mouth to stay shut for now, though the words I want to say to this bitch are nearly choking me. Pushing by her, I try for the exit.

"Do you really think your white trash self can just walk away from me? Nobody walks away from me," she snarls to my back.

I should have seen it coming, and in New York, on *my* turf, I would have. Even after our earlier confrontation, here in this expensive town with its expensive people, I didn't expect ghetto rules.

Two hands shove hard on my shoulder blades just as I see a foot shoot out from the table closest to me, and down I go. The cafeteria switches from silence to hilarity instantly, the loudest of the laughter coming from Hali herself.

Judging by the stinging pain and the taste of copper filling my mouth, I bit my tongue pretty damn hard when I hit, and the palms of my hands and my knees are going to hurt like hell tomorrow after slamming to the ground to break my fall.

Payne sticks his head back into the cafeteria and sees me on all fours with blood smeared across my lips, Hali standing over me looking like she just won some kind of prize. I watch as he grabs Sunday from the hall, and they move to my rescue. Lifting my chin and locking eyes with each of them in turn, I shake my head almost imperceptibly until they pick up on what I'm asking and stop moving toward me.

Slowly pushing myself to my feet and wiping my stinging palms on my skirt, I turn to face the bully behind me. She tries to cover her surprise at my audacity, but I recognize it. Like how dare I not be bawling and running from the room right now?

Yeah, well, fuck that and fuck her.

She doesn't deserve my tears, and she's got no idea who she's dealing with. In the grand scheme of asshole behavior directed my way, this doesn't even make the top twenty. It does irritate the hell out of me, though, and fuck me, does my tongue sting.

Expressionless, I step slowly and purposefully forward until I'm close enough to smell her baby hooker perfume mixing with what she ate for lunch, and I lean in and spit in her face.

The room goes dead silent.

Hali jerks her head back and inhales sharply. Standing there with my bloody saliva running down her smooth cheek, she turns an ugly shade of angry red and looks like she might actually reach out and strangle me right here in front of everybody.

Hands grab my arms from behind, and Sunday yanks me out of throttling range, herding me quickly and silently toward the exit where Roxy and Aylie are waiting. She's literally vibrating and shaking the entire way, and I can't figure out why, for the life of me. It's like she's angry at me, but every time I try to ask her, all she does is shush me coldly under her breath.

Behind us, Raff, Payne, and Heller form a wall, smiling jovially at a seething but still motionless Hali like nothing ever happened, preventing her from following me out should she regain her faculties anytime soon.

As I'm tugged past Poe, his arms crossed over his chest and his back leaning casually against the cafeteria door frame, he gives me a look of aggravation, tempered by a strange glimmer of something I can't put my finger on. Choosing not to dwell on whatever his problem with me is right now, I let the girls steer me to the nearest restroom to get cleaned up and inspect the damage done to my tongue.

Aylie throws open the restroom door so that the other two can push me through. Once inside, she pulls it closed behind us and plants herself in front of it like a cute little auburn-haired sentry. Yanking my arms free, I turn and face all three of them.

"What the hell, guys?" I throw my hands in the air incredulously. "You're not talking to me now? Are you mad at me? You know I had to do something, right? I couldn't just let her get away with tripping me like that!" The pressure in the back of my throat tells me tears are imminent, but instead of being born out of frustration, these come from a deeper place. A place I can't believe these girls have already started to wheedle their way into.

Sunday's face cracks like an egg, and she practically screams with laughter. Roxy adds her high-pitched squeal to the mix. I stand open-mouthed, staring at the two of them like they just grew extra heads. Swinging my eyes over to where Aylie still stands guarding the door, I see she's grinning and giggling too.

"That was the best fucking thing ever!" Managing to suck in a breath through her laughter, Sunday high fives Roxy and comes over to throw her arms around me. "Like ever, ever."

"Seriously, Stella, even though Hali has deserved that and more for a long-ass time, nobody would ever dare do what you just did. She's a heinous bitch if you cross her." Roxy shoves Sunday out of the way and hugs me. "That was truly beautiful—Miss Bitchface California standing in the middle of the cafeteria with bloody spit running down her face!" Roxy's words set both her and Sunday off into peals of laughter again, and I grin crookedly in return.

"Sorry you thought we were mad, Stell," Aylie offers, the petite redhead coming over to join us and patting my forearm, "we just wanted to get you away from there before she lost her shit and did something truly terrible, or before a teacher showed up and dragged you away to the headmistress." That's twice that she's made reference to something ominous being done by Hali.

What could she possibly have done?

Dismissing it for now, I rinse my mouth at the sink and see my tongue is still in one piece and has stopped bleeding. Turning to look at the others, part of me that has been

72

empty for so long fills with the glow of friendship being offered.

All of a sudden, the restroom door slams open, connecting solidly with the wall behind it and making us all jump. Expecting to see Hali, ready to stab me in the face with her lunch fork, I'm utterly shocked when Poe strides angrily into the room.

"Ladies," he growls. "Out. Now." He locks his predatory gaze with mine. "Not you, Bradleigh. You stay."

"Dude, you know this is the *girls'* restroom, right?" Sunday follows her question with a pointed look at Poe's crotch.

"I'm aware. I also don't care. Need to have a few words with your girl here." He's maintained a laser focus on me since walking in the room, almost daring me to be the first to look away. Which, of course, there is no way I'm doing.

"It's okay, Sunday. You guys go, and I'll meet you in class." I reassure them without averting my eyes, and they reluctantly make their way out into the hall, wanting to give me privacy but also desperately curious to know what's going on.

Poe and I hold our positions in silence for a minute or so longer until he finally breaks the staring contest with me and saunters over to boost himself up on the counter holding the sinks. Running his long fingers through his thick, espresso-dark hair, he clicks his tongue softly at me from his perch as a few strands fall forward, partially covering one eye.

Oh, shit. Is it hot in here?

My thighs start to tingle.

"Stella Bradleigh." My name drips like sin from his perfect lips. "How nice to actually meet you, especially after you so recently had your tongue down my throat," he chuckles. "Speaking of which, how is your tongue? I wouldn't want to see it permanently damaged before I know *fully* what it can do." I feel my cheeks pinken in frustration, though he seems to think it's for another reason. "No need to be embarrassed, kitten. That was the best service I've ever gotten in an airport. And I didn't even have to pay extra for it." Frustration quickly flares to anger. Now he's getting under my skin in a whole different way, the arrogant prick.

"You'd best tread carefully, Poe. This kitten has claws." I cross my arms, giving the underside of one a little pinch to keep my head in the game as he bares his perfect teeth in a grin. Tucking the corner of his full lower lip between those pearly whites, he slowly and tantalizingly lets it slide out.

An invisible anticipatory shudder runs through my entire body.

His grin widens.

Okay, so maybe not *totally* invisible.

Pushing himself off the edge of the counter, he moves slowly and intentionally toward me. My brain is telling me to back away, to run, but my stupid feet refuse to move. He stops a handbreadth away from me, cocking his head slightly as he studies my face. Once again, our gazes lock as I tilt my chin up in defiance, and he reaches out a hand to trail a finger over my cheekbone and down my jaw.

"No, not a kitten, are you?" He pauses, and so does my pulse. "A star. With eyes like a summer night just before dawn." Suddenly, both of his strong hands reach down and grip my waist. Before I can blink, he lifts me effortlessly and spins us around, depositing me in his vacant spot on the countertop. Tangling his fingers in my long hair and leaning down, he quickly captures my mouth with his, stealing my breath and wrapping me in the scent that is so uniquely him.

When his tongue gently twines with mine, there is no pain from my earlier injury, only a warm, wet heat that builds in my center. Wanting more, my hands reach up of their own accord to thread through his silky hair, pulling him closer.

Oh God, I've never tasted anything as good as Poe's lips.

Trailing his hands from the ends of my hair, down my sides, and across my thighs, his fingers grip my knees tightly and shove my legs apart, making me gasp into his mouth. Breaking our kiss, he holds my gaze steady and drops to his knees on the floor in front of me. The current of need running through my veins is almost painfully unbearable, and I let my head fall back as he hooks his strong forearms under my bare thighs and pulls me closer to him. The granite of the counter cold against my flushed bare legs, I lean back on one hand and fist the other against my mouth. As he feathers his lips teasingly over the sensitive skin on the inside of one knee, I can feel myself starting to squirm and wanting to moan loudly.

Pushing my school-issued skirt higher, his breath is warm and almost reverent on my most sensitive area, still covered by my now soaking wet, and probably see-through, delicate white lace panties. Brushing his lips softly over the dampness, I can feel his mouth move into his familiar little smirk.

"Star?" he whispers, pulling back slightly and leaving me aching at his absence.

"Mmm? Yeah?" I mumble, eyes closed and voice thick with desire.

"Stay away from Hali."

What did he just say?

My eyes fly open in disbelief as Poe gets fluidly to his feet. With a very naughty wink, he licks his lips as he strolls out of the restroom, leaving me sitting on the counter, unsatisfied, with my legs splayed and my breathing heavy.

I'll say it again for those in the back row. What. The. Fuck?

Sliding off the counter as Poe did earlier, I attempt to collect myself, quickly adjusting my skirt and fixing my smeared lip gloss, all while trying to pretend I don't see the tears of frustration welling in my reflection's eyes. With his head between *my* fucking legs, he brings up *her* name? Is this some kind of fucked up payback for the airport?

As my lust fades and leaves me shaking, my anger surges. My last thought before pulling open the restroom door is that Poe Halliday is going to fucking pay for what he just did. He wants to play games? Bring it on.

CHAPTER NINE

By the time I get to class and slide into the empty seat next to Sunday, I've managed to get myself under some semblance of control, and to the average observer, I probably look completely normal. To anybody who knows me though, the slight pink flush high on my cheekbones and the small tight smile that doesn't show any teeth are dead giveaways that my urge to punch somebody in the face is strong.

Sunday eyeballs me appraisingly for a few seconds, then rummages through her bag and leans over with a hair elastic pinched between two fingers. A knowing grin on her face, she glances quickly at my head and shakes hers. Snatching the elastic from her hand, I quickly bundle my long dark hair into a messy high ponytail and subtly raise my middle finger at her in thanks. Blowing me a kiss like the sarcastic ass I'm learning she is, she turns her attention back to the front of the room, leaving me to quietly hatch over-elaborate revenge plots involving parts of Poe's anatomy and sharp cutting tools.

Finally, the next period bell rings, and I'm happy to escape to music class. I can tell Sunday is dying to know the details of what happened in the restroom after her, Roxy, and Aylie were ejected, but her questions will have to wait. To be honest, I'm okay with that right now. I just want to enjoy the relative peace of my last class of the day and go back to my aunt's.

The first thing I notice when I walk into the music room is that there are quite a few more people in it than there were yesterday. The second thing I notice is that Roxy is in this class too, and she sees me at almost the same time.

"Hey! We finally have a class together!" Excitedly, she motions me over to the empty seat beside her, and I grin. Roxy seems like the type to approach everything exuberantly, and I both envy that and am grateful to be included in it. Just being around her makes people smile.

We spend the next few minutes talking about each other's musical influences and Roxy's family's involvement in the industry, which has me more than a little envious. And though she skirts the issue briefly once or twice, she's considerate enough not to just come right out and ask what happened with Poe. It's a relief to be able to have a relatively drama-free conversation, and Roxy seems like a decent human, so I'm happy to count her as another friend.

My calm is short-lived, however.

"How nice of you to join us, Mr. Halliday." The portly music teacher greets him with the tone of an exasperated man who knows he can't do a damn thing about it, and gets up to close the music room door behind the late arrival.

My head swivels away from Roxy and toward the front of the class, where Poe stands surveying the room. Either the disbelief or the annoyance plainly visible on my face must be like catnip to him because, of course, he goes straight for the empty seats behind Roxy and me.

Seriously, Universe, why do you have it in for me? I ask silently toward the ceiling. *What the shit did I ever do to you?*

Gritting my teeth in seething frustration for forty-five minutes straight, I keep my head forward and focus as best I can on the lesson, which is difficult since Poe's mere presence seems to suck all the air out of the room.

Picking up on the connection between the jackass lounging casually in his seat with one arm draped over the back of it and the pulsing twitch in my clenched jaw muscles, Roxy does me a huge solid and runs interference without me even asking. As soon as the last bell rings, she nudges me toward the door and turns the full force of her perkiness on an unsuspecting Poe, peppering him with questions about the upcoming gala, his parents, and surprisingly, Heller.

Making my hasty escape, I beeline straight for my locker. Hurrying to get everything into my bag that I need for the mountain of homework I plan to scale this evening, I nearly jump out of my skin when I feel a hand on my upper arm. Spinning on my heel, ready to smack whoever the hand is attached to, I pause in confusion at the clean-cut face staring back at me.

"Hi? Did you need something?" I ask the blond quarterback-next-door standing with his hands up and a generically pleasant smile on his face.

"It's Stella, right?" He lowers his hands slowly. "Didn't mean to frighten you."

"Don't worry about it. It takes more than that to scare me. Who are you again?"

Let's hurry this along, champ. I need to get out of here.

"Bingham Ramsey, captain of the varsity football team. I'd like to offer to be the head of your welcoming committee." Another pleasant smile, this time accompanied by a short laugh and a hand offered to me. Tentatively, I reach out and shake it. His grip is limp and as bland as his smile. "So, there's a party on Saturday…"

The rest of his sentence is lost on me as Poe rounds the corner and purposely slows his roll as he approaches Bingham and me.

Dammit.

Thinking fast, I reach out and rest my hand on the quarterback's arm, laughing at whatever inane comment he just made. My arrow hits home as Poe's brow darkens into a scowl, and he picks up his pace and noisily shoves his way through the parking lot doors. Bingham steps slightly left into my line of sight, effectively blocking the exit from my view.

"You want to go then? What time should I come by?" Startled back to the conversation, I look at him questioningly.

"Sorry, what?" I ask. "I think I missed that last bit?"

"Saturday night. Roxy Rose's party? What time do you want me to pick you up?"

Something about this guy is tickling my creep detector, but I can't put my finger on what it is. Did I really just agree to go to Roxy's party with him when I wasn't paying attention? Not wanting to be rude, I play along.

Damn you, Poe, and your annoyingly distracting self.

"Nine o'clock, I guess? Ten? What time do parties get started around here?" I ask with a shrug. Bingham smiles, seemingly pleased, but the smile doesn't quite reach his eyes.

"Pick you up at nine." He turns, with that slightly off-putting bland-but-still-blinding smile on his Malibu Ken face, and walks off toward the exit.

"Uh, don't you need my ad—" I start. Cutting me off with a wave over his shoulder, he laughs and answers without turning around.

"Everybody knows where you live, Stella," and then he's out the door, leaving me staring after him feeling a little sideswiped.

Squeezing my eyes shut and shaking my head to clear the brain fog Bland Bingham left behind, I realize I'm now late for meeting up with Sunday to grab a ride home. I slam my locker shut, the noise echoing in the nearly empty hallway, and sprint out to the equally nearly empty parking lot.

The scene that greets me has me snickering and somehow sweeps away the day's bullshit in one shot. Sunday is lying on the hood of her Range Rover, back against the windshield, with her signature pink sunglasses on. That in itself wouldn't be so bad, but the windows are all down with 50 Cent's 'P.I.M.P.' playing on the stereo, and her seriously off-key sing-along has me in stitches.

"You weren't kidding about your vocal abilities, were you?" I poke as I walk up to the car.

"You're just jealous that I can look this damn good while sounding so damn bad," she grins without turning her head toward me. I toss my bag in the backseat through the open window and climb up on the hood, settling in beside her. "So, Stellaaaaaaaaaaa," she drags my name out, still grinning and still not turning her head, "have fun in the restroom today?"

"In the name of all that is holy, if I tell you what happened, will you please stop singing?" I plead, laughing and sticking my fingers in my ears for emphasis.

"You got yourself a deal there, missy!" With an elbow jab

in my ribs, she whips off her sunglasses and sits up cross-legged, turning her whole body to face me. Why do I have the feeling this isn't the first time Sunday has used her wretched singing voice to get her way?

Sighing, I resign myself to having to rehash all the sordid details of my bizarre-o restroom tryst, so I fold my arms across my stomach and close my eyes, enjoying the warmth of the late afternoon breeze. I stay in the same position for the next ten minutes—three minutes of me telling her what *and who* went down, and the remaining seven minutes of her cycling through glee, shock, anger, and declarations of righteous vengeance as any true girlfriend would. When both she and the playlist pumping out of the car stereo run out of steam, I crack an eyelid and glance over at her suspicious face.

"There's something else you're not telling me," she pouts.

Well, she's not wrong.

Figuring I might as well get it out into the open, I say it all at once.

"I think I agreed to go to Roxy's party with Malibu Ken, but Poe was walking by, and I was pissed at him and wasn't paying attention when Malibu asked, and that's the only reason I can think of that I would say yes, and now I have to go to the party with somebody I don't even know." My voice keeps getting higher, and Sunday's eyes keep getting wider as my sentence keeps getting longer.

We sit in silence for a few seconds; the breeze tickling through the trees the only sound around us in the now completely empty parking lot.

"Stell, who the hell is Malibu Ken?" At her question, I drop my head into my hands.

"He said his name was Bingham something," I confess, head down and voice muffled.

"Huh." Pause. "Bingham Ramsey?" Another pause. "Bingham Ramsey asked you to go to Roxy's party with him?" When I finally lift my head, I don't like the look I see on my friend's face. It too closely resembles the odd, vaguely creepy vibe I was feeling about him earlier.

"What? Is he an ax murderer?" I try to joke. When she doesn't answer me and just sort of frowns instead, I get apprehensive. "No, seriously, Sun, am I going to end up chopped into bitty bits by this guy? Is he going to want me to 'put the lotion on its skin'? I refuse to get Buffalo Bill-ed my first week here, so spill it, Easton!" I'm mentally cataloging how many different ways I know to take this Ramsey fucker down should the need arise when Sunday finally speaks.

"Ax murderer? No." She chews her lower lip pensively, looking like she's choosing her next words carefully. "There were some rumors last year. Nothing serious. But, Stell, really? Bingham Ramsey? Isn't he kind of, I don't know, icky?"

"Rumors about Malibu Ken? What kind of rumors?" A small nervous laugh escapes me. "He seems so bland. Like vanilla pudding. Or a mushy banana."

"Just be careful, okay, Stell? At least he's bringing you to Roxy's, so we'll all be there too." Trying to lighten the gray mood that's fallen over both of us, Sunday slides off the hood of the car. As she's getting into the driver's seat, she teasingly says, "I've seen him sniffing around Hali lately, so that speaks volumes about both his IQ and his taste in women. Wonder what that says about you?" She flutters her eyelashes at me, all innocent-like.

Flipping her the bird for the second time today, I climb off the car and into the passenger seat. I'm awarded the honor of choosing the music for the ride to my aunt's house, so I crank up the Deftones and spend the entire fifteen-minute drive wondering what Bingham Ramsey's deal is.

CHAPTER TEN

POE

My attitude manages to appear casually neutral for about three minutes after we walk into the cafeteria. Then Raff sits down right beside her, and for some fucked up reason, I want to throat punch him. Being the ass that he is, the bastard turns his megawatt charm on full force, knowing it will get to me, and flashes her the grin that has set legions of girls' panties on fire. The kick to his shin under the table and my brief glare sparks his laughter, but he shifts his attention away from her and starts arguing with Heller about cars instead.

When we finish eating, and Heller sets her back on her feet, we are out the door. I'm striding away, trying to put as much distance as possible between myself and temptation, when Payne hollers to hold up for a minute. He backtracks, following the swell of mocking teenage laughter tumbling through the cafeteria doors behind us.

Christ, what now?

He comes rushing back out and weighing his available options on the fly, grabs Sunday, pulling her back into the lunchroom with him. Curious now, and also somehow knowing whatever is going on in there is going to severely piss me off, I sidle up to the doorway just in time to see Stella spit directly in Hali's face.

My immediate reaction is to cheer and fist bump everybody in the room, but instead, I attempt to keep my face expressionless and lean back against the door frame, crossing my arms in front of my chest. Sunday and Roxy pretty much steamroll Stella out of the cafeteria, and as she passes me, blood smeared across her lower lip, it's all I can do to stop myself from reaching out and wiping it away from her gorgeous mouth. Once the girls are past me and out of sight, I walk up behind my three best friends who have taken it upon themselves to block Hali should she try to go after Stella. Hali's blustering and posturing stop as soon as she sees me coming, and her threats of violent retaliation turn to simpering pouts.

"Poe, did you see what that horrible girl did to me?" she whines, her fat crocodile tears imploring me to take her side. "All I did was ask her how she liked being here, and she got so upset she tripped and fell. Then she turned around and spit on me!" Sniffling and carefully wiping under her eyes to avoid smearing her makeup, she adds a little tremble to her lower lip for extra effect.

Unable to hold it in anymore, my laughter explodes like buckshot, and her oh so innocent façade cracks just a bit. Moving between Raff and Heller, I step to within an inch of her to make sure she gets the point.

"You're a fucking liar, Torsten. You know it, I know it, everybody in this room knows it." The façade falls away even more, and the flush of anger starts to stain her neck and cheeks a mottled red. "They're just all too chickenshit to stand up to you, and you're pissed that Bradleigh isn't."

"I don't know what you're talking about. Really, I don't."

She laughs, flipping her hair in a ridiculous attempt at nonchalance.

"There you go again. I think you've gotten so used to lying and manipulating everybody and everything around you that you don't even know what's real anymore. You actually believe your own bullshit, don't you?" Leaning in a little closer, I lower my voice further. "You and I will never be anything. Don't you get it yet?"

"Your mother might have something to say about that." She snarls back at me.

"Fuck what my mother wants. She's not the Heir. *I* am." Leaving her seething behind me, I turn and head for the doors, my friends following close behind. Frustration and anger are warring for dominance in me, and something snaps. Silencing the voice in the back of my mind telling me what a colossally bad idea this is, I switch direction midstride and cross the hall to the girls' restroom. Raff and Heller take up sentry points on either side of the door, and Payne just stands back, shaking his head and grinning. Shoving the door open, I find some perverse satisfaction in watching the four girls inside jump.

I push myself harder, feeling my arms and shoulders scream in protest at the extra chin-ups. Counting out the last seven, I let go and drop to the mat below. One of the perks of my family having more money than they knew what to do with was this ridiculously huge house with this insane workout space. I swear, my father's home gym is better equipped than most commercial ones, and he's never here to use it. Lying here, my back and chest damp with rivulets of sweat after an hour and a half of push-ups, sit-ups, and chin-ups, I wonder what she would look like laying here with me, covered in an entirely different kind of sweat.

Dammit. I knew toying with her this afternoon was a bad fucking idea.

Groaning loudly, I shift as my dick reacts to the thought of her damp, naked skin.

My thoughts are interrupted by doors slamming and glass smashing in the kitchen. Steeling myself for what I know is to come, I haul myself up and pad barefoot down the hall. I arrive just in time to hear my mother ripping into Marisol, our cook, for some imagined slight and rummaging through the walk-in pantry like she knows what she's doing. Leaning against the counter and crossing my arms, I give the frightened cook a wink.

"Mother, what exactly is the problem this time?" I ask. She leaves the pantry at the sound of my voice and pats her hair to make sure it hasn't gotten mussed during her tantrum.

"You would not believe the incompetence that's running rampant in this house." She turns on the cook cowering against the island. "You. Are you trying to poison me? How dare you try to serve this garbage?" She gestures to the pot simmering on the stove that's filling the air with a delicious smell.

"Ma-a-a-m," the small woman stammers, "You asked f—" Her sentence abruptly ends when Eunice Halliday's hand snakes out and slaps her hard across the face, the crack echoing in the cavernous kitchen.

"Mother! Enough!" I step in between the two women, tucking the now crying cook behind me. Staring down the woman who gave birth to me, I can see her weighing the option of smacking me too, just for getting in the way. Drawing in a long-suffering breath, she instead flicks us away with her blood-red claws and stalks out of the room, sulking because her tirade got interrupted.

"Thank you, Poe," Marisol wipes her eyes quickly, embarrassed at crying in front of me. "Your mother is very angry today." Offering a commiserating half-smile, I pat her on the shoulder on my way out of the room.

"When is she *not* angry? Let me go shower and change, and I'll be down for dinner, okay?" She nods gratefully and starts cleaning up the mess my mother made.

I climb the winding stairs to my room in the east wing, each hollow footstep reminding me of how empty this house truly is. Oh sure, there are people here: Marisol, Javier, my mother's saint of a driver, Hendrick, my father's valet when he's home and the house butler when he's not, and a brigade of maids and gardeners. But there is no love here, no joy. My mother makes sure to drown it all in Glenlivet or Grey Goose, and my father uses business as an excuse to stay as far away from her as possible.

When I was younger, I used to wonder why my parents were together since, even then, I could tell they didn't like each other. Now I understand it's more of a business deal, and just the way the founding families do things, but there is an undercurrent between them that carries something darker. An air of sadness lives in my father that he tries to keep hidden, and my mother is just a vicious, drunk socialite who likes to throw the Halliday name and money around.

Slamming my bedroom door shut behind me, I strip my gray joggers and boxers off as I walk, and kick them in the direction of the closet. My phone connects automatically to the wireless Sonos system, and I step into the oversized glass shower to Bring Me the Horizon's 'MANTRA' streaming through the speakers.

With the hot spray pounding against my neck and back, my thoughts turn to a pair of stunningly violet-blue eyes, luscious tits, and a perfect pussy covered by lacy white panties.

Poe Halliday, you are one stupid fucker. One tiny taste, and now you're hooked. Fuck it. Fuck that. Maybe a release is all I need to get her out of my head.

Leaning forward slightly, I plant the palm of one hand flat against the shower wall, while the other reaches down and firmly grasps the full wood I'm now sporting. Remembering how her soft curves felt molded to my hard planes at the airport, my hand starts to move. Remembering her damp panties clinging to her slit gets my hand moving faster until the thought of her warm, wet mouth wrapped around my dick has me throwing my head back, and I come hard, shooting all over the tiles in front of me.

Breathing heavily, I close my eyes and duck my head entirely under the running water, enjoying the feel of it against my skin, but knowing it's a poor substitute for her hands tracing lazy paths down my chest. A burst of agonized laughter escapes me.

Well, that didn't work. She's still all I think about. This girl is going to drive me insane.

Thoroughly irritated now, I shut off the water, make a half-assed attempt to dry off, pull on some jeans and a hoodie, and head downstairs for dinner.

My mother has apparently decided to forego solid food this evening, likely in favor of her preferred liquid diet. Marisol offers to set a place for me in the elegant formal dining room, but I quickly put a kibosh on that, choosing instead to eat in the brightly lit kitchen while she chatters to me about her kids.

Out of nowhere, a shriek of fury penetrates the bubble of pleasant calm I had been enjoying. Marisol's eyes go wide with fear, so I get up and go meet Satan herself as she barrels down the hall clutching her drink, giving the kindly cook time to escape.

"Did you think I wouldn't find out?" The blistering rage in my mother's eyes is something to behold, primarily because it has to be some kind of scientific marvel that they don't explode in their sockets from the sheer force of her anger.

"Find out what, Mother?" I sigh.

"Don't play stupid with me, boy. You know exactly what I'm talking about." She stops for a few mouthfuls of her dirty martini. "There is a Bradleigh Heir in Folkestone again."

I knew she was going to flip out.

"Oh? There is? I hadn't noticed," I try to pretend I have no idea what she's talking about, the dread starting to seep into me. "Anyway, so what if there is? What does it matter?" Jamming my hands in the front pocket of my hoodie, I brace myself for her answer.

"You're just like your father. A spineless, sniveling waste of skin, sniffing around a Bradleigh skirt." Her tone is barbed and laced with loathing, and she actually spits when she speaks. She's so mad and so drunk. "You should have been the one to tell me, so we could devise a plan to drive her out, just like her whore of a mother." I flinch internally but keep my stare blank and my spine steel. "Instead, I had to hear it from Callum Torsten. At least he and his daughter understand what loyalty means." She drains the last of her drink and stumbles only slightly on her way for a refill.

"And what exactly *does* loyalty mean, Mother?" I ask her retreating back, regretting my words the second they leave my mouth.

Fuck. You know better than that. Don't engage the piss-drunk shrew.

She stops and turns to face me slowly, her expression blank, and for a minute, I think I might get out of this unscathed.

But only for a minute.

"You dare to question me?" Raging again, her face pinches and twists, and her steps pick up speed and purpose as she strides toward me. I hold my ground, refusing to give an inch to this vile, hateful woman. "You will follow the plan. You will respect me as the only person in this family with the ability to do what's needed. And you *will* keep your dick out of the Bradleigh trash. I will see to that."

With her bloodshot eyes narrowed in hate and her teeth bared in a terrifying mockery of a smile, she slams her empty glass down on the small table beside us, shattering it into glittering pieces. One slices directly into the palm of her hand, and she gives no indication that she even knows it's there. Snarling her disgust at me one last time, she turns away, swaying toward her wing of the house and leaving tiny droplets of blood in her wake.

She will see to that? What the fuck does that mean, and why does it make my skin crawl?

My car took the brunt of last night's shitty sleep on the drive to school this morning. Slamming through the gears and disobeying pretty much every traffic signal, stop sign, and speed limit, I'm surprised I didn't end up wrapped around a tree.

"Damn, bro, what happened to you? You look like shit." Payne falls into step beside me as I walk through the main doors.

"Don't even get me started," I growl, shooting him a dark glare.

"That look must mean Eunice was in rare form when you got home," he says knowingly. Out of all the guys, Payne is the one most familiar with the toxic flame-thrower that is my mother. He's also the only one who has any idea she exists primarily on hate, plastic surgery, and booze.

Grunting my agreement, I catch sight of glossy raven-dark hair alongside angelic silvery blonde moving in our direction through the crowd of students. Turning to my locker, head down, I hear Sunday's chatter and Stella's answering laugh as they pass behind me. My hand fumbles with the combination lock as the warmth of just hearing her voice floods through my veins.

Fuck fuck fuck! When did I turn into such a needy asshole? I feel like a twelve-year-old with his first hard-on every time she's anywhere near me, and half the time when she's not.

Pounding the side of my fist against the metal door hard enough to leave a slight dent, I close my eyes and force myself to calm down.

"So. You going to tell me what that's all about?" Payne leans his head back against the locker right next to mine, staring at the ceiling as he waits for me to answer.

"Can I be honest?" My oldest friend doesn't shift his position at all, just gives me a quick side-eye like I'm asking a ridiculous question I already know the answer to. It makes me grin a little. "What do you know about the history between the Halliday and Bradleigh families?" I ask, careful to keep my voice low. Adjusting his position to allow us to speak a little more privately, he answers in equally low tones.

"Probably the same things you do. Up until our parents' generation, the Bradleighs were the top dogs, and the Hallidays were their closest friends and allies. Isaac and Annah Bradleigh had two daughters, Catherine and Cecily, with Catherine chosen as the Heir. Some bad shit went down, and she disappeared, leaving her parents heartbroken and her family in tatters. I've heard my parents speculate that she never actually left. That she died in some gruesome way, and Isaac covered it up. Nobody seems to know the real story, though with New Girl showing up, it looks like the disappearance angle is more likely." He shrugs.

"Totally agree with you on that. Catherine left here alive." I bite my lower lip, something about the whole thing bugging me.

"All the founding families live by the same rule: once you're designated the Heir, you wear that title until it passes down to your child on their eighteenth birthday. Not knowing what happened to Catherine, Cecily couldn't and probably wouldn't take over the role when her sister disappeared. Without an Heir, the Bradleigh rule ended, and the Hallidays became the top of the food chain." Payne finishes and waits for me to spit out the thought I'm chewing over.

"There's more to it. I'm positive. My mother has always made it crystal clear how the Bradleighs deserved to be destroyed. She practically foams at the mouth just hearing their name. Then, about three years ago, she started pushing hard for an alliance between our family and the Torstens." I run my fingers through my hair, leaving unruly spikes, and Payne whistles softly through his teeth.

"Jesus, Poe. You and Hali? That's a horrifying fucking thought." He shudders visibly at the idea.

"No shit. I have nightmares about being shackled to the venomous bitch. One night when Mommy Dearest was drunker than I ever remember seeing her, I asked her why she was so hell-bent on me marrying Hali. She started mumbling about loyalty and an old debt before she passed out." My hand curls into a fist, and vomit crawls up my throat in disgust at the thought of fucking Hali to produce the next Heir.

"Last night, Eunice found out about Stella being in Folkestone, and legit lost it, right?" Payne rubs the back of his neck thoughtfully. "That tells me she knows Stella is for sure Catherine's daughter and will take on the role of the Bradleigh Heir as soon as she turns eighteen."

"And my bitch of a mother is determined to drive her out of town before that can happen."

CHAPTER ELEVEN

Thankfully, the remainder of the school week is mostly uneventful. The four of us girls eat lunch together both days, and the guys join us as well.

Sunday, Roxy, and Aylie have all gone out of their way to make me feel as comfortable as possible in this alterna-verse I've walked into, and I'm more grateful to them than I could ever explain. Without them, I likely would have cut and run after my first day.

The guys seem to have welcomed me into their circle too, with the glaring exception of Poe. He *has* gone out of his way, but only to avoid me since the little Bingham incident in the hallway on Wednesday afternoon. Every time I see him, I alternate between wanting to jump on him and sink into that sinful mouth of his, or throat punch him for being such a prick to me. He sits with us at lunch, but at the opposite end of the table, as far away from me as possible. Every once in a while, though, I catch him watching me when he thinks I can't see him, and my pulse stutters at the mixture of hunger and anger swirling in his eyes.

I've come to the conclusion that Poe Halliday is impossible and more fucked up than even I am, and I should just get used to him hating me and move on. Of course, that's my logical brain talking, and neither my heart nor the rest of my body gives a shit about what I *should* do. Plus, I still owe him for that little oral stunt he pulled in the restroom the other day.

By the time Friday afternoon rolls around, I'm tired and fidgety and so ready for this week to be over. Luckily, word of my spitting incident in the cafeteria hasn't made it back to Cecily yet, and I'm proud of myself for not taking it further and knocking Hali flat on her ass.

Exercising that kind of restraint deserves some weekend party fun, right?

Sunday drops me off after school, only letting me leave the car after I renew my promise to go shopping with her the next morning. I don't have the cash to spend on new clothes, but I can window-shop and keep her company.

Taking the stairs to my room two at a time, I huck my bag into the cavernous closet, wincing at the thought of the pile of homework I have stowed in it and telling myself that I'll get to it later. I dig a pair of denim cut-offs and my only bikini top out, and after changing and tying my thick dark hair up into a messy bun, I head downstairs in search of my aunt. The kitchen is empty, but the giant sliding glass doors are open to the pool deck and the grounds, so I wander outside and find Cecily on a lounge chair at the poolside. She looks up from her magazine as I approach and tosses it on the small table beside her, giving me a big grin.

"Ah yes, returned from the trenches, I see. How goes the battle?" she asks, tongue firmly in cheek. Dropping into the lounge chair beside her, I loudly puff out a lung-full of air through my pursed lips.

"It's going to take me forever to get caught up in my

classes. I'm really trying, and I think my teachers recognize that, but there is a lot of work, especially if I want to go to college after I graduate. *If* I graduate." I add a little dejectedly. Reaching over between the chairs, Cecily pats my arm reassuringly.

"You'll graduate. You're a smart girl. Of that, I have no doubt."

The Pacific Coast sunshine warms my pale New York skin as I lie back in my chair. With October only a week away, back home, the persistent humidity of the summer will be gone, and the chilly nights will be settling in.

I wonder if I'll miss that. Fall in New York is beautiful.

We sit in companionable silence for a few minutes, listening to the lazy hum of a faraway lawnmower and the chuckle of the waterfall as it spills into the pool.

"Cecily?"

"Mmmmmm?"

"Do you know the Hallidays?" I feel my aunt tense. She's quiet for a few beats, and I'm not sure she's going to answer me. When she finally does speak, her careful words are in a purposely neutral tone that I've not heard from her before.

"Why do you ask?"

I clear my throat, uncomfortable now but not sure why.

"No real reason, I guess." I shrug one shoulder dismissively. "I'm sort of making friends, so I was just wondering if you knew his family." My attempt at mild disinterest might not be playing out as well as I'd hoped, so I tell myself to just keep breathing calmly.

"Who are your new friends?" she asks, deftly avoiding my initial question.

"Well, you know Sunday already. Then there's Roxy Rose and Aylie Claire. The girls have all been great. The guys in the group are Heller Jackson, Payne Emerson, and Raff Essex." I pause. She snorts.

"And?"

"And Poe Halliday," I add reluctantly.

"I forget how much you don't know about your family and this town." She whispers, almost to herself. Not wanting her to stop talking, I sit quietly and wait for her to continue. After a minute or so of thought, she sighs and sits up, swinging her legs over the side of her lounge chair and turning to face me.

"The founding families are all represented here now. Easton, Rose, Claire, Emerson, Essex, Jackson, Halliday, and now Bradleigh," she says softly, almost reverently. My brow draws down in confusion.

"Founding families?" I question. "What do you mean by *founding* exactly? And why do you say *and now Bradleigh*? You've been here the whole time." I can feel my chest getting tighter.

"They are the first families, the families who built this town and everything in it. For a long time, there hasn't been a Bradleigh Heir in Folkestone or at Woodington. Your mother was gone. She was the Heir, and now that title falls to you when you turn eighteen next month." Cecily smiles sadly, almost in apology. "There is another family who has tried very hard to fill that void over the years, but most of the other founders won't have anything to do with them. They consider them interlopers and see them for the vicious, status-seeking, malevolent individuals they are." She pauses. "Now that you're here, the circle is complete again for the first time in almost twenty years."

I'm not entirely sure how I feel about being a member of a founding family.

What the hell does that entail? Does it come with a crown or a tiara or something?

I laugh at the thought of me walking around like a pageant girl, doing the queen's wave, and wearing some atrocious satin nightmare of a dress.

"Do you get along with all of them?" my aunt asks, taking a long swallow from her water bottle while keeping her eyes locked on my face.

"All except Poe," I answer honestly. "He and I, there's something weird there. Oil and water or fire and ice." Just thinking about what happened on Wednesday after lunch gets me riled up again. "The arrogant ass pretty much goes out of his way to avoid me most of the time, which is fine by me. Though he did offer me a bizarre warning the other day."

Yeah, bizarre in both the message and the delivery method, alright.

My aunt is instantly concerned.

"Warning? What do you mean *warning*?" Cecily looks a little pale around the edges of her honeyed tan. A bit *too* pale for a trivial high school threat from a shithead guy. I start absentmindedly nibbling on my thumbnail.

"Nothing serious, he just told me to stay away from another student. A nasty bitch named Hali."

At that, some of the tension leaves my aunt's face and she laughs, the sound thick with irony.

"A Halliday warned you to stay away from a Torsten?" She laughs even harder, her sides shaking and tears forming in her eyes. Staring at her like she's just gone off either her rocker or her meds, I wait for her to calm down before I speak again.

"Care to share with the class? What's so funny?"

"Sorry." She wipes her eyes with the corner of her beach

towel. "It's just funny that he would warn you away from the one girl who is closest to his family. Or closest to his mother, anyway. Hali Torsten's parents are the ones who have been trying to fill the Bradleigh hole in our little town. And Eunice Halliday, Poe's mother, has been their strongest supporter ever since day one."

That little tidbit of information gives me a jolt.

So Poe and Hali? Is that why he warned me away? To keep her from finding out about what happened at the airport? But then why tell me with his head between my legs? I mean, that seems pretty counter-intuitive.

I know Sunday said Poe ignores Hali fully and completely, but there have to be things that she doesn't know about.

"Just be careful, please, Stella. The world here is very different from the one you were raised in. Things often aren't what they seem, and what seems like a minor issue can escalate very quickly." Standing and gathering her towel and water bottle, Cecily lays her hand on my shoulder. "Something happened in that group to scare your mother badly enough to leave and go into hiding, and I would hate to have history repeat itself."

With a last squeeze, she drops her hand and makes her way back into the house, leaving me alone by the pool, lost in thought.

Saturday dawns rainy and cool. I left my window open a little last night, and the first ten minutes of my morning is spent cuddled into my pillow mountain listening to the soft patter of raindrops through the trees and the occasional grumble of thunder in the distance. I desperately want to stay in my cozy little nest, but I promised Sunday I would go shopping with her, and I'm nothing if not a woman of my word.

Cecily meets me in the kitchen after I'm showered, dressed, and halfway through my cereal.

"Big plans today?" she asks, leaning against the counter while she waits for her coffee to finish brewing.

"There's a party at Roxy's tonight, so Sunday is dragging me shopping with her." I shrug. "I figure keeping her company while she looks for the perfect outfit is the least I can do after she's been so great since I got here." Leaving out the part about my going with Bingham tonight, I finish the last of my cereal and get up to rinse my bowl and shove it in the dishwasher.

"What about *your* perfect outfit?"

"I don't think I'm going to get away with worn-in jeans and my oversized hoodie." Chuckling, I join Cecily back at the table. "I brought my black T-shirt dress with me, so that'll do. As I'm sure you've noticed, I'm not exactly overly concerned with the latest fashion trends."

The two of us simply sit together for a few minutes, watching through the glass sliders as the finches chase each other around the trees in the yard. The side-eye my aunt is giving me is nearly burning a hole in my temple, but I'm choosing to pretend I don't notice it, knowing full well this will likely be the only quiet I get all day and not wanting to spoil it. Sunday was way too excited about our shopping trip today, so her level of chill will likely be non-existent.

Finally, Cecily abandons her beloved morning coffee and disappears down the hall, returning a few minutes later with a black plastic card in her hand. Setting it in front of me, she sits back down and starts drinking her coffee again, a small pleased smile on her lips. Pushing the card away in protest does no good as she just slides it right back to me.

"This is yours," she says, an indulgent note in her voice. My face must be broadcasting my discomfort because she laughs and gives me a mock stern look in return. "It's not unlimited, so maybe don't go trying to buy a Ferrari or a leopard or anything." I try to object again, but she's not having any of it. "You should've been doing this your whole life, Stella. This money is yours, too. You are the Bradleigh Heir, after all."

There's that Heir thing again. Auntie and I are going to have a little sit-down about what precisely that means soon.

"Buy yourself some new clothes and anything else you need. Have fun. Be young for once." She stands and pats my shoulder, and I reach up, putting my hand over hers in silent thanks. Embarrassed, I keep my head down as my eyes glaze with unshed tears at the kindness this woman continues to show me.

Cecily heads off to get ready for her day while I sit and stare at the black card still on the table in front of me. This all feels like some weird dream.

Is this really my life now?

Even though I still don't know the rules or what any of this means, I'm starting to like my aunt a lot, and my new friends seem pretty great, so why not go with it? Everything has been a struggle for so long, and a lonely one at that, so why shouldn't I enjoy my new life?

It can't be any worse than the one I seem to be leaving behind. Right?

CHAPTER TWELVE

*M*y phone chimes with a text message letting me know that my ride is out front. It's just a selfie of Sunday crossing her eyes and sticking out her tongue while flipping the deuces, but I get the gist. Laughing, I grab the credit card and shove it in my back pocket, along with my phone, and head out to the Rover after yelling goodbye to Cecily.

"What up, homie?" she laughs, nearly yelling to be heard over Post Malone.

"You're crazy, lady!" I grin as she turns 'A Thousand Bad Times' even louder, and we pass through the gates at the end of the driveway.

Five exhausting hours later, I feel like I ran a marathon. If shopping were an Olympic sport, Sunday would medal in it every damn time. I'm used to working ten-hour shifts at The Juneberry, and I still couldn't keep up.

Somewhere in my sore-feet-induced haze, I agree to let

Sunday help me get ready for the party tonight. When we get back to Tweedvale and unload our bags into my room, we head out to the pool for a quick swim before dinner. In my case, it's more of a float in the shallow end, since I'm not entirely sure my spaghetti arms and legs would stop me from drowning at this point.

Cecily calls us in for dinner and over huge Cobb salads, she asks about the party tonight. Of course, the blabber-mouth sitting across from me lets it slip that I'm not going with her, but with Bingham Ramsey. Her shin is an easy target for my kick under the table. I roll my eyes when she gives me her innocent bystander look, which is completely ruined by the smart-ass grin that follows, tucking the corner of her mouth into her cheek.

She tries to hide it, but I catch the same strange look cross my aunt's face that showed up on Sunday's when I told her about my date the other day.

"Does somebody want to tell me what's going on? Like, should I not be going with this guy?" Cecily and Sunday look at each other across the table.

"He doesn't strike me as your type. I thought you'd be going with somebody else if you weren't going to go with the girls, that is." She stares into space for a few seconds, lost in her own head as her salad fork taps her front teeth gently, before she tunes back in and smiles at both of us. "Oh well, I'm just glad you're going to Roxy's and that the girls will be there, too. You can all keep an eye on each other." Curious about who she thought I'd be going with, but not really wanting to ask her, I drop it and let Sunday drag me upstairs to play dress up.

Here's where our differences become glaringly obvious. The first thing *I* do is sit cross-legged on my fluffy duvet and find some music for us to listen to. The first thing

Sunday does is throw open the walk-in closet doors and start rooting through my shopping bags. I set my phone in the dock of my little stereo and lean back, 'Last Resort & Spa' by Battle Tapes playing through the speakers as I watch Sunday put my new clothes away with a fair amount of amusement on my part.

"Sunday, why are you hanging up my clothes? You know I'm perfectly capable of doing that myself, right?" She just rolls her eyes like I asked the dumbest question ever.

"How else am I going to see what your outfit choices are? Stell, I'm an artiste," she jokes. "This is my palette. Let the master create." With a theatrical flourish, she thumbs her nose at me and steps back to consider the options.

It's taken less than a week for me to learn I should just let Sunday do her thing when she's on a roll, so I find myself relaxing, enjoying the music and the puffy pillows and soft bed. I seriously love this bed. It's like a big, warm, comfy hug. My eyes drift shut, listening to the faint mutterings and musings coming from the other side of the room.

Sunday lands beside me with an *oomph,* having taken a running jump from somewhere near the middle of the room and making me bounce before she drapes herself across my legs.

"Okay, you. I have the perfect outfit picked out. Are you going to make this easy, or are you going to be difficult?"

Jesus, how bad is it if she's asking me that before I've even seen what she chose?

Suspicious now, I scoot up to a sitting position, rubbing my fists into my eyes. With a sigh, I drop my hands into my lap.

"Dude, what are you trying to get me to wear, and why do I think I'm not going to want to wear it?"

"Promise you won't argue? Just take my professional

word for it and wear what I picked for you?" She gives me the biggest puppy dog eyes I've ever seen.

"Your professional word? Are you trying to dress me up like a baby hooker?" I ask with a nervous laugh, mostly kidding, but a little concerned I might be right. Her eyes widen in mock horror, her hand covering her heart.

"Moi? I would *never*. Shut yo' mouth." Performing a hilarious and freakishly agile commando roll off the bed and jogging over to the closet, she pulls out her chosen pieces. My mouth falls open, fully ready to protest, but before I can get a sound out, she's already crossed back over to me and dropped everything on the bed.

"Pllllleaaase, Stell?" She gives me her best dramatic pout, paired with a quivering lower lip, so I really can't refuse her. But maybe I can get something out of this, too?

"I'll make you a deal. You can dress me up however you like if you agree to tell me more about the whole founding family bullshit. You know, since you neglected to mention that you, Roxy, and Aylie are the queens of this town, as much as the guys are the kings and all." Arms crossed, I stare at her accusingly.

"Is that all?" She waves her hand dismissively. "That's easy. We can totally have story time while we nurse our hangovers tomorrow. Sound good?"

Much to her glee and against my better judgment, I agree. Sunday runs with it, like a hyperactive kid given a pound of candy and eight sodas, even going so far as electing herself my hair and makeup department as well. But, by the time both of us are ready, I have to admit, she's good at this. I know I'm decent-looking, but I've never looked like *this* before.

"Holy shit, girl. You are hot. Like hot, hot. Poe is going to shit his pants twice tonight."

"Twice?"

"Yes, ma'am. Once when he sees your seriously fine ass in that outfit, and once when he realizes Bingham Ramsey is your date." Pleased with her handiwork, she packs up her own purchases from today while I tidy the vanity in my ensuite bathroom quickly. I've always been a drugstore mascara and lip gloss girl, and now there has to be at least twenty different products on my counter that I'm pretty sure I will never remember how to use.

While I'm cleaning up, I realize that if Sunday's right about Poe's reaction to both my ass and my date, I can use it to my advantage.

Maybe it's time for a little game of 'Make the Jackass Jealous'.

Dabbing a little of my new perfume on the pulse points at my neck and wrists, I take one last look at myself in the full-length mirror and shake my head, still not sure how I got here.

As I step back into my room, Cecily knocks on the door to let us know Bingham is here to pick me up. Sunday and I trundle down the stairs, each of us loaded down with the bags of clothes and shoes and makeup she bought today, when she stops briefly at the front door and reaches her hand out for my arm.

"Stell, just so you know, I wasn't trying to hide what I am, or my place in this shitty town. It really doesn't mean much to me, and if I could leave it all behind, I would. You're so new to all of this, and I didn't want to scare you away with the weight of what your name signed you up for the minute you got on that plane. Please don't be mad." She looks so worried, and her words are so sincere.

"No worries, Sun. We're good." Her face breaks into a relieved grin, and we load her bags into the back of the Rover as Cecily comes down the front steps.

"You look beautiful, girls. Have fun tonight. Watch out for each other," she whispers into my ear as she gives me a hug goodbye. Bingham leans casually against the passenger door of his white BMW sedan, so I make my way over to him. Before getting in, I wave at Sunday as she drives off, and blow Cecily a kiss as she reminds my ride to drive carefully. Once we're on the road, Bingham glances over and gives me a quick up and down.

"You look good." There is something hungry about his expression that I'm not entirely comfortable with.

"Thanks." My smile is tight. We're quiet for the rest of the drive to Roxy's, the air in the car stale and dry, just like the guy behind the wheel. I spend the whole time wishing I had just gone with my girlfriends, and trying to ignore the way Bingham keeps licking his lips and slanting his eyes in my direction.

Pulling up to Roxy's house, I'm in awe. The massive stone and glass structure emanates light from every window, and I'm pretty sure you can see it from space. Even crazier, the triple-wide, curving drive is lined on both sides with what has to be millions of dollars' of wet-dream-worthy vehicles. My stomach starts to do its clenchy thing and panic runs her sharp, cold fingernail down the back of my neck.

Calm down. You are Stella Evangeline Bradleigh, whatever the hell that actually means. Right here, right now, that name is a magic pass saying you belong here, at least for tonight. You are not party crashing, and you don't need to worry about getting caught somewhere you shouldn't be.

Bingham parks and gets out, coming around to my side of the car but not opening the door for me.

Uh, okay. This guy is odd. Who stands there like that and doesn't open the door?

The moment gets more awkward the longer it draws out, and I've finally had enough, so I suck in a deep breath and open the passenger door myself, stepping out into the driveway. The clueless oaf ignores me on the walk up to the front entrance, and the closer we get, the more I'm kicking myself for agreeing to be Bingham's date.

Just as I've decided to ditch Malibu Ken the minute we get inside and worry about finding another ride back to my aunt's later, the front door opens, and a few drunk rich boys spill onto the porch. Suddenly Bingham's big sweaty hand is gripping mine, and he's practically dragging me along behind him, making a show of our entrance. Not appreciating being anybody's hood ornament, I wrench my hand away with a dirty look in his direction and catch something lurking behind his typically bland expression that gives me the shivers.

Distancing myself from this guy right now seems like the best idea in the world, so I start threading my way deeper into the house on my own, head down, hoping to find one of my friends.

"You shouldn't ever walk with your head down, darlin'. That face is too pretty to hide." Raff slides smoothly up beside me, his green eyes twinkling, and the sideways grin he gives me makes me feel instantly better.

"Aww, shucks, Raff. You make a girl blush," I joke and playfully butt my shoulder into his arm. He throws the same arm over my shoulders in a big brotherly way and takes a pull from his beer.

"Come on, New Girl, let's go see what kind of trouble we can get into." I laugh, and he offers me a swig of his drink as we spot Sunday and Aylie, working our way over to them.

"Hey, hottie!" Sunday winks and blows me a kiss. "Where's Malibu Ken?"

"Anywhere other than here would be preferable. That guy is kind of an ass." Aylie nods her agreement, and color floods her cheeks when Raff turns his attention to her, a look of confusion on his handsome face.

"Who is Malibu Ken, Ayls?" he stage-whispers at her.

"Bingham Ramsey. He brought Stella here tonight." Raff almost chokes on his mouthful of beer and Sunday pounces.

"See?! There is something with that guy!" She points her finger accusingly at Raff. "Rafferty Essex, spill it!"

"I barely know the guy. But I *do* know somebody who is going to be pissed when he finds out who Stella came with." He shakes his head and laughs wryly. "Sun, maybe you should give her room in your Uber after the party, so she doesn't have to ride home with Captain Dipshit." In complete agreement, I nod at Sunday vigorously, my hands steepled together pleadingly.

"Your wish is my command," she jokes. "Duh, of course you can catch a ride with Aylie and me. Not even a question." Breathing out a sigh of relief, I mouth a silent thank you to her, to which she winks back with a grin.

The four of us stay together, a strange little island of privacy in the noise of the party until Roxy and Heller join us. Roxy squeals when she sees me and wraps me in a hug hello. Raff leans over and says something in Heller's ear that makes the blond guy's eyes widen slightly before narrowing back toward where Bingham and I came in. Heller nods once, apparently agreeing with whatever Raff just told him. When he sees me watching, his handsome surfer boy face breaks into a smile.

"Looking tasty, New Girl." He leans over and gives me a peck on the cheek. "Who needs a drink?" All four of us girls raise our hands, and Raff and Heller mockingly curtsy at us before heading to the kitchen.

As the girls chat around me, I have a chance to take in my surroundings. Roxy's house is beautiful. A blend of what looks like an original building of stone, with expansions and additions of modern glass and metal, it's something that I can appreciate. I like the idea of the new being added without erasing the old, and even embracing it. As I'm admiring the house, I notice how we four seem to have a buffer of space around us that isn't afforded to any other group here. Almost like the other party-goers are keeping a respectful distance. I wonder if that's got something to do with the founding families thing Cecily was talking about. There's no time to ask, though, as the guys show up with drinks in hand and Payne and Poe in tow.

Okay, now things will get interesting.

Raff hands me a red Solo cup, and Payne tips his beer to me in a toast.

"Glad you came, Stell." Tapping cups, we both take long swallows and grin at each other when we come up for air.

Poe, the asshole, simply pretends I'm wallpaper and sits down in the large armchair, watching everything around him like a king surveying his subjects.

Dammit! How the hell am I supposed to get this guy riled up when he won't even look at me?

Irritated as much by his arrogance as by the fact that he continues to ignore my existence, I resist the urge to stamp my foot and scream in his face like a bratty kid. Instead, I ask Roxy for the way to the nearest bathroom.

"Don't use the ones down here." She points to the illuminated glass and iron staircase leading to the second floor. "Go and use mine upstairs; down the hall, third door on the left. People here know the rules—nobody upstairs at my parties unless specifically invited. Way more private up there."

Fascinated by the all-glass risers, I take my time climbing the stairs, which is probably a good thing given the height of these heels Sunday insisted I wear. I find my way to the door Roxy directed me to and open it into her bedroom.

Holy shit.

The room my aunt gave me is big, but Roxy's bedroom is at least twice the size and more like a suite, complete with a small sitting room and a wood-burning fireplace. Something familiar about the wooden mantle above the stone fireplace catches my eye and draws me over to it. Running my hands along the carved flourishes and roses, I recognize the same craftsmanship and feel of both the box my aunt sent me and my closet doors.

That's odd. Isn't it? That the same person seems to have made them? Do all the founding families have something made by him?

I'm so lost in my thoughts that I don't even notice I'm no longer alone until it's too late.

CHAPTER THIRTEEN

A strong forearm wrapped in ink curls around my waist, and a low voice whispers next to my ear.

"I thought you came upstairs to use the bathroom, Star." My entire body is instantly hyperaware of how close Poe is standing behind me. The feeling is magnetic, and I allow myself the briefest of moments to lean back into his warmth and breathe in his scent. He chuckles, a satisfied rumble low in his throat, and I jerk away, moving a good five feet from him to avoid further temptation. He sets his half-empty beer bottle on Roxy's mantle and leans back against the wall, thumbs hooked in the front pockets of his almost-black jeans. Watching me with his lazy half-smile, that damn piece of hair falls over one eye again, and my pulse stutters at how fucking sexy he looks.

"I did. I am. Can you leave, please?" I spit back at him.

"Nah. I'm good right here."

Why is it every time this guy pays any attention to me, it involves a fucking bathroom?

"Fine. Whatever." Rolling my eyes, I stomp over to the attached bathroom, making sure to lock the door behind me. I actually don't even have to pee, I just had to get away from the party for a minute, and now I just want to get away from Poe. I *need* to get away from him. Sitting down on the closed toilet seat lid, I wonder how long I'll have to stay in here before he leaves. Frustrated, I pull out my phone, make sure the volume is off, and find some stupid match-three game to play to pass the time.

After about five minutes, there are sounds of movement in the sitting room, and relief floods my senses, tinged with something that *might* be disappointment.

Thank fuck, he's finally leaving and going back to the party.

Suddenly the bathroom door handle jiggles, followed by a loud click, and the door swings open. Poe sees me sitting there, playing on my phone, and furrows his brow, silently judging me.

"What? Never had a girl disappear to the bathroom to get away from you before?" I ask, shrugging my shoulders. "Also, I know I locked that door." My scowling at the offending lock makes him laugh.

"We've all been friends since birth. Every one of us guys has been able to pick this lock since we were ten. The girls used to use this as a hiding spot during hide-and-seek until we figured out how to get the lock open."

Sighing in frustration, I stand, cranky now. Moving to the sink to wash my hands, I try to focus on anything other than how the snug black Henley molds to his muscular chest and lean waist, and how his dark jeans sit low on his hips.

Stopitstopitstopit.

Leaning into the mirror above the sink and pretending to check my makeup, I catch his eyes hungrily roving over my bare back and down my long legs. The clinging black jersey top Sunday picked out for me may have long sleeves and a flattering but modest scoop neckline in the front, but the back drapes delicately from my shoulders into a deep V. With my long hair up in an elegant twist, most of my back is exposed, from the nape of my neck, down almost to my waist. His eyes climb back up and meet mine in the mirror.

With the fluidity of a prowling cat, Poe is suddenly directly behind me, and my breath catches. Never once breaking eye contact with me in the mirror, he reaches out and runs the fingers of one hand slowly down my spine, sending shivers to every part of my body. I leave my hands, palms down, on the counter, unable to stop myself from wanting to see where this goes. My four-inch black stilettos leave me about two inches shy of Poe's usually daunting height, and I have to admit, I'm enjoying the more level playing field.

Still maintaining eye contact, I can see his mouth curve into a dangerous grin as he realizes I'm not backing down. Enclosing both of his arms around me, his strong hands find and pop open the button of my curve-hugging butter-soft black leather pants and slowly drag the zipper down. My breathing gets faster, and I bite the side of my lower lip. Still, I refuse to release his gaze as he slowly slides both hands into the sides of my pants and pushes them down just enough to expose the hot pink lace panties underneath. He swallows hard, and his tongue slides out across his lower lip, flashing the stud piercing it.

We stand like that in silence for a few seconds, staring at each other in the mirror and daring each other to be the first to give in. I raise an eyebrow teasingly and move my hips ever so slightly, rubbing my still partially leather-clad ass against him. With a groan I choose to interpret as defeat, he closes his eyes and leans his head back.

Two can tease, Halliday. I win this round.

Smirking, I reach to fix my pants and zip them back up when he presses tightly against me and grabs my hands, planting them back on the vanity in front of us, the heat in his eyes telling me silently not to move.

Uh-oh. I might have underestimated the game a little bit.

He removes his hands from mine and skims them softly down my sides, sending goosebumps chasing each other across my arms. Grabbing my hips firmly, he yanks backward, repositioning me so I'm not fully bent over, but my ass is sticking out, and I'm definitely leaning into my hands on the counter. He grasps the waist of my pants and slides them down my legs, letting them pool at my ankles and trailing soft wet kisses up the backs of my bare legs as he stands.

My heart is hammering so hard I'm surprised it's still in my chest, and the wetness between my legs is warm and slick. Reaching around me again, Poe slides one hand up under my shirt, and I'm suddenly reminded I'm not wearing a bra. Palming my left breast and holding its weight in his palm, his thumb and forefinger find my hardened nipple and roll it between them before giving it a little pinch. The moan that escapes me is quiet but deep, and I see him smile in the mirror. Moving between both nipples with the same hand now, he continues to roll and pinch and lightly flick them, one after the other, while his free hand reaches under the waistband of my flimsy panties and slides into the wetness between my legs. Hearing his appreciative purr in my ear when he finds me bare and smooth almost pushes me over the edge. Then both of his hands are gone, and I cringe as I wait for him to drop another cryptic comment on me and disappear like last time. But no, he's got something else in store for me tonight.

Dropping to his knees, he positions himself between me

and the vanity. I move my hands to his broad shoulders as he reaches up and hooks a finger around the soaked front of my panties and pulls them to one side. Looking up at me and grinning like the devil himself, he reaches out with his other hand and spreads the softest part of me with the tips of his fingers. When his tongue flutters over my exposed clit, my knees shake and nearly buckle at how fucking amazing it feels.

Closing my eyes, I grip his shoulders to keep from losing my balance and revel in the feel of his pierced tongue, licking and sucking at the hard little button between my legs. Something about not being able to spread my legs fully, with my pants still around my ankles, makes the sensations utterly different than what I'm used to. The orgasm builds like a hurricane, faster and harder than any I've felt before.

"Poe," I pant, "Poe, oh my God."

"You like that, Star?" he asks between flicks of his tongue. "You like the way I lick you?" Hearing him talk like that pushes me even closer to the edge. Digging my fingers in so hard that I know he'll have crescent-shaped nail marks as a reminder, I try my best not to scream in ecstasy.

"You are so fucking beautiful like this. Come for me, Star." With those words, I break apart harder than I ever have. The orgasm rolls over me in waves as Poe's tongue works its way deeper, riding the surge with me and lapping up my wetness.

Once I can stand on my own again, I let go of his shoulders, and he carefully lets my panties fall back into place. Wiping his chin discreetly on the inside of my thigh, he places a soft kiss on the sensitive skin. As he stands, he slides my pants back up my legs, his deft fingers zipping and buttoning them closed. Standing there, in Roxy's bathroom, nearly eye level with each other, I feel like something's changed. The air around us is supercharged as he leans his forehead down against mine.

"This isn't good, Star. This is dangerous." He raises his head and kisses my forehead with a tenderness I had no idea was possible from him.

"Dangerous?" I ask, confused.

Stepping back without answering me, he reaches for my hand and pulls me into Roxy's sitting room. He stops to retrieve his beer bottle from the mantle and turns to face me at the door, uncertainty wreathing his gorgeous face. Letting go of my hand, he runs the back of his knuckles across my cheekbone, and I close my eyes, relishing the electricity generated by his skin against mine.

He opens the door, and we head down the hall together slowly, lingering as our hands brush against each other on our way to the top of the stairs. Poe starts down first, and when he stops abruptly halfway, I misstep trying not to run into him and roll my ankle slightly in these ridiculously high heels.

"Poe? Jeez, you need brake lights back here if you're going to stop like that." Grinning, I put my hand on his back, and he shrugs it off immediately as if I burned him. When he swivels his head in my direction, the clear blue of his sapphire eyes moments ago is murky with stormy dark clouds. He laughs, mirthless and cold, loud enough for the partiers nearest the stairs to listen.

"You didn't think that bit of action meant anything, did you?" He smirks and takes a pull of his beer. "Sorry, sweetheart, I'm not into trash. You may have the last name, but you're a whore just like your mother, and you don't belong here." Looking me over, head to toe, with a disgusted look on his face, he delivers his harshest blow. "You aren't good for anything more than kneeling on a bathroom floor with my dick down your throat."

Recoiling like he punched me in the face, and with horror and confusion threatening to choke me, the searing heat of my rage quickly dries any tears that might have been sparked by his lies and bullshit comments.

What the fuck? Why is he lying? He's the one who was on his knees! And did he seriously just call my mother a whore?

"I don't know who the fuck you think you are or what gives you the right to talk shit about my mother, but stay the hell away from me, you shitty, arrogant, lying prick. When you're done playing emotional terrorist, go find somebody else to fuck with because I'm done." My sore ankle temporarily forgotten, I make sure my fist connects with his crotch as I shove by him to get down the stairs. "By the way, acting like a dick won't make yours any bigger, fuckface." As I get to the main floor, I notice Hali standing just off to the side with her hellions, well within earshot of what just happened, looking satisfied and laughing cruelly, her lips twisted in a mocking pout.

Madder than I've ever been and absolutely gutted, I resist the urge to physically remove the shit-eating smirk from her face, and settle for stomping the stiletto heel of my shoe into her exposed toes on my way past. Her shriek of pain does nothing to make me feel better about what just happened, but it's satisfying nonetheless.

It's a toss-up right now whether I'm angrier at him for being a douchebag of epic proportions, or myself for letting my guard down, and all I want right now is an escape.

All the rich assholes crammed in here make this huge house seem more claustrophobic than any shithole single-room apartment back in New York. This new life, these new people, and Poe's emotional hit and runs have all combined into a seething mess of rage and pain and sorrow. Feeling utterly heartbroken, I allow it to combust.

Welcome to the self-destructive, bad decision portion of our program, ladies and gentlemen. You are a stupid, sappy girl at heart, Stella Bradleigh, and that's why it was just ripped out of your chest and set on fire in front of most of the senior class. Thank you very much, let's get fucking wasted.

Avoiding Sunday and the rest of the Heirs, I go in search of the kegs, only to find Raff refilling his cup at the tap. Quickly reversing course on sight, I'm not quite quick enough; he follows and reaches out to grab me with a big grin.

"New Girl! What's the hurry? What're we doing?" Jerking away, I stare straight into his brilliant green eyes.

"Fuck off, Raff." The smile vanishes from his face. As I turn to leave, he reaches out again.

"Stella. What happened?" Grabbing his beer from his hand, I move out of his reach and choose to ignore the genuine look of concern he's giving me. Instead I opt to back away into the crowd with my chin up and my face a stony mask. No matter how hard I work to keep my eyes blank though, I know flickers of pain are dancing through their depths, and if I stare at Raff too long, he's bound to see them. Refusing to expose any more of myself to the vultures, I spin on my heel and disappear into the crowd of people using Roxy's living room as an impromptu dance floor.

CHAPTER FOURTEEN

POE

*U*sually, I'm down for a party, especially when it's one of us throwing it. My mood has been so shitty lately though that I'd love to skip this one, but I can't. The guys wouldn't care if I told them I wanted to sit this one out, but they aren't the reason I'm going. She is. I don't know if she'll actually be there, but on the off chance she is, I need to see her, be near her, even if I have to pretend to hate her.

The past couple of days have been challenging for me. After my run-in with Hali in the cafeteria, she's been particularly loathsome, somehow ending up wherever I am and making her presence known. Always laughing too loudly at stupid shit or rubbing her tits against me when she walks by. I've started having the guys show up everywhere ahead of me and texting me if she's there. I would avoid the cafeteria altogether, but I know it's the one place I have an excuse to be around Stella, even though I keep my distance.

Moving through the halls, I can always feel when she's near. It's like something in me recognizes its equal in her and wants to pull us together. I know I'm making her feel like shit, hell, I'm making *me* feel like shit, but it's how it has to be. It's safer for her this way. Every time my need to apologize to her for being such an ass and to ask if we can start over tries to overwhelm me, I remind myself of my mother's creepy as fuck threat, and I force myself to keep my distance.

It's almost ten o'clock when Payne texts me and asks if I'm still planning on driving tonight. Knowing there is no way I'm staying in, I text him back that I'm on my way.

Pulling on dark jeans and a fitted black Henley, I run some product through my hair and spray on some cologne, telling myself I always go to this much trouble when I go out.

Sure you do, fucknuts.

Slipping on the large hammered silver ring that belonged to my grandfather, I jam some cash and my license in my back pocket, grab my keys and phone, and jog down the stairs out to the garage.

One thing I have in common with my father is our love of cars. Five of the bays in our six-car garage are outfitted with hydraulic lifts so we can fit a total of eleven vehicles in here. My ridiculous mother refuses to ride in anything other than her chauffeur-driven limo, so the single is for her. The other ten spots are for my father's toys and my car.

I push the wall button to open my bay door and slide behind the wheel of my black Aston Martin Vantage AMR, an eighteenth birthday gift from my father, and feel a little of my stress ease as the engine growls to life. Dropping it into gear, I make the short drive to the Emerson estate in silence, enjoying the rumble and purr surrounding me.

"Well, don't you smell nice, princess?" Payne razzes me as he climbs in.

"You looking to walk to the party, jackass?" I fire back, a little more bitingly than I intended.

"Oh, shut up and drive, Halliday. Don't fuck up my night because you have a raging case of blue balls." Laughing, he flicks through my playlist and cranks up 'Can You Hear Me' by Korn.

Bro, if you only knew how much more than blue balls it really is.

Roxy's place is on the other side of our small town. My nerves are making me antsy and my foot heavy on the gas pedal, so the ordinarily fifteen-minute drive takes only eight. Whenever the Heirs throw parties, we always make sure to set aside preferred parking for the others, either to avoid being boxed in or to have a place to leave our cars overnight if we decide to drink. Pulling into my usual spot, Payne stops me before I get out.

"You really have a thing for her, don't you?" he asks in a voice that lets me know he's serious.

"Yeah, I do. And fuck if I know what to do about it."

I love Roxy's house. It's smaller than mine, but the melding of stone, glass, and metal has always appealed to me. When I was younger, and my mother would get blind drunk and start smashing shit at home, I would often bike to the Rose's house, and Roxy and I would watch movies while her mom would stuff us with junk food. This place has always been a haven for me.

Walking in through the front door, we head straight for the kitchen and the kegs. Threading through the crowd, I don't see the face I'm looking for, and the one I'm actively avoiding plants herself directly in front of me.

"Poe, you came." Hali looks like she's ready to hit an L.A. nightclub or a stripper pole. Hair in perfect waves, thick fake eyelashes, eyebrows drawn on, and covered in that weird shimmery highlighter shit certain girls seem to love. And all of it wrapped in a red leather halter dress short enough to require a second hairdo.

Before I can say a word, Raff's voice pipes up as he and Heller materialize behind me.

"Fuck off, Hali."

"I wasn't talking to you, Rafferty." She snarls at him.

"Don't care who you were talking to. Sentiment stays the same. Fuck off, Hali." The way he says it, with his big grin and cheerful voice, is just so *Raff*. Hali looks at me, seeming to expect me to ask her to stay, and when I just stare back at her with a bored expression, she gets seriously pissed and flounces off.

"You'd better watch it with that one," Heller warns, finishing off his drink. "I have a feeling she could get pretty fucking nuts, pretty fucking fast." Payne and I glance at each other, and I sigh.

"You're not wrong, bro. You are so not wrong. I need a fucking drink." The four of us finally get to the kegs, and as I dip into the secret stash of bottles Roxy keeps for me when we party here, I notice Raff filling three cups, then Heller filling three more.

"Jesus, Raff, you guys going on a bender tonight?" I ask as I crack open the top on my beer.

"Not that you'd recognize it, but we're gentlemen, Halliday. Fetching drinks for the womenfolk." I snap my bottle cap between my fingers, aiming for his head.

"That's for calling me unrefined, dick."

"Don't let Sunday hear you refer to her as womenfolk. She'll kick your ass." Payne says with a grin and elbows

Heller, jostling his arm.

"Watch it, fucker. If you make me spill her beer, I'll tell her *you* called her womenfolk, and she'll kick your ass twice as hard."

While I'm listening to my friends' banter, my brain suddenly registers four extra beers, not the usual three. The uptick in my pulse has me wanting to kick my own ass.

She came.

"Who do you think would win in a fight, Sunday or Payne?" Raff asks as we follow him and Heller back to where the girls are waiting for their drinks.

"Sunday." All of us, including Payne, answer in unison without hesitation, unable to stop the laughter that follows.

"Alright, alright, what about New Girl or Poe?"

"Shut the fu—" Midway through my thought, the crowd parts, and I have a clear line of sight to the girl in question, and my mouth goes dry as my dick twitches to life.

Sweet fuck, that is the single hottest female I have ever seen.

Standing with the other three, Stella is the only thing I can focus on. She's magnetic. All of that silky, dark hair twisted up on top of her head, her striking violet-blue eyes lined softly, and wearing curve-hugging black leather pants that look like they were tailor-made for her. She turns to answer a question from Sunday, and that simple move awards me a perfect view of the deep V in her top that exposes most of the pale, creamy skin of her back.

"You okay, brother?" Payne hangs back beside me, knowing full well what's got my attention. He claps his hand on my shoulder, and I turn to look at him, letting him see the pain and turmoil written all over my face. He whistles softly. "What are you going to do?"

"The only thing I can." Carefully arranging a disinterested mask over my features, I join the rest of my friends,

Payne following close behind. Sinking into the nearest chair, I survey the room, looking everywhere but at her as I try to drink my beer calmly. The fucked-up thing is I can feel her frustration and hurt at the way I'm ignoring her, and it bothers me. A lot. My friends and I are the kings of Fuck and Chuck. No strings, no seconds, and no apologies. I've ignored tons of girls over the years. Hell, I do it to Hali every day, and it doesn't bother me in the slightest. Seeing Stella upset though twists like a knife in my gut, and knowing I'm the cause of it nearly breaks my resolve.

From the corner of my eye, I watch her abruptly get up from the arm of Sunday's chair and hear her ask Roxy where the bathroom is. When I see her push her way through the crowd to the stairs leading to the second floor, I finally release the breath I feel like I've been holding since we got here.

"Hey, have you guys seen Malibu Ken anywhere?" Sunday asks, looking around the room. "I need to go kick him in the junk." Choking on my saliva for a minute, I cough to clear my throat.

"Sun, who the hell is Malibu Ken, and why do you need to inflict damage on his junk?" My confusion only increases when I look over at Raff and see him counting down from five on his fingers.

"That's Stella's nickname for Bingham Ramsey. He brought her here tonight and made her feel super shitty. I feel the need to return the favor." Raff counts his last finger just as my fist tightens around the neck of my bottle, and my jaw clenches in anger.

"See, Sun? I told you I knew somebody who would be pissed off." He just grins at me when I pin him with a glare. Shoving out of my chair hard enough to move it back a few inches on the carpet, I ignore the stares I'm sure my reaction is getting and follow Stella upstairs.

Advancing quietly down the hall to Roxy's room, I pause in the open doorway and watch Stella caress the hand-carved wooden mantel above the fireplace. Even that simple movement is so fluid, so graceful.

And so damn erotic.

She must not have heard me coming down the hall, or she'd be grabbing the closest thing available to throw at my head.

Even though I know this beautiful, brave, and sinfully sexy girl in front of me can never be mine, something in me craves everything about her. Tonight, I just need to know what it would feel like if things were different. To touch her creamy skin. To hear her sigh my name. To taste her.

You are so fucked, Halliday. So very fucked.

My willpower crumbles under the weight of my need. Crossing the room silently, I step up behind her to curl my arm around her waist, whispering low next to her ear.

The taste of her still on my lips, I stomp my foot harder on the gas pedal as I rip through the gears and push the speedometer up over 100 miles per hour, racing the back roads toward the coast. Northlane's 'Bloodline' raging from the speakers and the wind whipping through the wide-open windows do nothing to ease the lump of guilt and shame sitting in my stomach.

"FUCK!" Pounding the steering wheel, I scream into the wind, devastated by the look on her face that will haunt me until the day I die. The look *I* caused, with empty, vicious words meant to keep her safe. But she doesn't know that. All she knows is that she trusted some fuckstick with an intimate part of herself, and he tore her to shreds in front of a live audience.

Nearly losing it on the last turn before the dirt road leading to the hidden beach the guys and I found when we were younger finally forces me to slow down. This small, sheltered section of sand and ocean has been our place to escape to for years.

Pulling into the parking area we created under the trees, I shut off the ignition and climb out, taking the two six-packs I grabbed from Roxy's fridge with me. The light of the moon is more than enough to show me the path down to the water. I kick my boots off awkwardly as I stumble my way to sit on the sand with my back to the pile of driftwood we use as a makeshift shelter. Twisting the top off a bottle, I finish it in five quick swallows, tossing the empty and opening the next one.

What have I done?

Gulping down the second and third bottles in rapid succession, I set them aside and rest my forehead on my knees, hands tugging at my hair as I replay the gut-wrenching scene on the stairs. I had no intention of leaving her like that, no intention of destroying her. As soon as I started down those stairs, still high on her allowing me to give her that leg-shaking orgasm, Hali's livid face at the edge of the crowd told me the bitch had an idea of what just happened. The promise of retribution written all over it scared the shit out of me.

Because it looked just like my mother's face.

And it wasn't aimed at me.

It was aimed straight at Stella.

So, I did the only thing I could think of; I made sure she'll hate me, throwing my mother's words about *her* mother in her face. Watching her walk away from me almost made me puke, and I thundered down the stairs needing to get the hell out, only to have my escape intercepted by Hali as she followed me outside. When she reached out and touched me, I lost it. Ripping my arm away from her grasp, I looked her straight in the face and called her every filthy expletive that came to mind, before getting in my car and peeling out.

The breeze coming off the dark water is cold, chilling the tears streaking my face and making me curl in on myself even further. Finishing the rest of the beer in my hand, I wonder drunkenly if Stella's okay and finally pass out on the sand, with dreams of her screaming my name haunting me.

CHAPTER FIFTEEN

*F*inding my way to the backyard without further incident or interruption, I drag a patio chair into a darkened corner to finally sit down and try to digest what happened inside. The emotions Poe keeps fanning in me are volatile and confusing.

How can a person switch gears so fast? How can he kiss me so tenderly one minute, and then publicly and horrifically humiliate me the next?

Unfortunately, my mulling over of recent events doesn't have a chance to go any further as Malibu Ken steps toward me from the shadows beyond the pool house.

"Hey. Where have you been?" Bingham asks. Still too wired and upset by what happened with Poe, his blunt question tangles in my already over-sensitized nerves.

"Does it matter? I'm here now, aren't I?" A slow smile spreads across his face at my clipped response, making him look like a creepy wax version of himself with the way the shadows are playing against his features.

"You want some company?" he asks. After another long

swallow of the beer I stole from Raff, I set the half-empty cup on the small glass table beside me. I drop my head in my hands and take a deep breath.

"Sure. Whatever." I mumble through my fingers. His heavy steps move closer to the pool, where he grabs another chair and drags it to my position, the metal feet grating over the stone pool deck. I keep my face buried in my hands a little while longer, not trusting myself to not burst into tears quite yet.

Here in the relative quiet of the Rose's expansive yard, I can hear my thoughts without the noise of a hundred other voices taking up space. Lifting my head and tilting it all the way back, I stare at the clear night sky and, for the thousandth time, wonder what the fuck I'm doing here in this town, at this party, in these clothes.

Bingham hums quietly beside me, and I take a deep breath, turning to face him. He picks up my red Solo cup and dangles it out to me, almost challenging me to finish it. Glancing down into the pale amber liquid, I have a quick internal battle. Should I stay and try to have some fun, or should I call myself an Uber and go back to Tweedvale to feel sorry for myself?

Screw it. Why shouldn't I have a little fun after Poe and his bullshit? Might as well live up to my trashy reputation.

"Cheers," Bingham says, his eyes hooded in shadows as he taps his cup to mine." I raise my cup and tip it back, draining most of it in two gulps. The alcohol burns its way down my throat and into my belly, leaving a tingling warmth behind.

Bingham leans back in his chair, and we sit, and he talks. And talks. About football, his car, his plan to take over the world. Okay, that last one probably isn't entirely accurate, but I feel a little fuzzy around the edges, and I'm not fully listening to him anymore. As his lips continue to flap, his empty eyes watch my every move, and I'm not sure he ever actually blinks. Like a snake. Giggling to myself at the comparison, I slide low enough in the chair to rest my head against the back, and the reflection of the house lights dancing off the swimming pool entrances me.

I don't know how long I sit like that before I notice Bingham has stopped speaking and is watching me silently.

Waiting.

Waiting? Where did that thought come from?

Giving my head and arms a bit of a shake, I stand a little too quickly and wobble unsteadily.

"Looks like that beer hit you harder than you expected, huh?" Playing the role of Good Samaritan, Bingham puts his beefy arm around my shoulders and pulls me tightly to his side. Too tightly for my liking. But when I try to pull away, I realize my limbs don't seem to be under my control anymore. Digging his fingers into my upper arm, he steers me toward the path leading around the side of the house.

The bones in my legs are turning to mush. I can't feel my feet, and somewhere along the path, I lose one of my pretty new shoes. In my foggy brain, I picture Sunday's face when I tell her I only have one shoe left, and for some reason, the thought makes me laugh, a hollow, faraway sound to my ears. My head lolls on Bingham's shoulder; it feels thick and seven sizes too large for my tiny straw-like neck to support.

He keeps half-tugging, half-shoving me along until we reach the passenger door of his BMW. As he struggles to keep me upright and get the door open at the same time, it briefly registers in my short-circuiting brain that we're leaving the party.

Why are we leaving the party?

"Malibuwherewegoin'?" I slur, my words like sticky taffy and my tongue an old wool sock.

"Who the fuck is Malibu?" The sharp, icy voice cuts through my blur enough for me to register that I should be worried, but not enough for me to remember why. The door is whipped open by a faceless hand, and Bingham dumps me in the front seat with a grunt before slamming the door shut again.

Resting my temple against the tinted glass of the side window, I hear muffled voices outside the car, and the sound almost lulls me to sleep before he opens the driver's side door and slides behind the steering wheel. Practically laying on top of me, he reaches across my body for the seat belt, buckling me in and giving it a yank to make sure it's secure.

God, that's awful. Old gym socks and stale beer and frustration.

The smell coming off of Bingham makes my stomach pitch and roll. My eyelids are heavy enough that they might as well be sewn shut, so I feel rather than see his cold hand roughly graze the side of my face before reaching up and pulling the pins from my hair, its inky darkness falling around my shoulders. After rubbing a soft lock of my hair between his fingers, he gives it a hard tug, making me grunt in protest. His response is to reach hungrily for my breast and twist my nipple hard enough through my shirt to make me scream.

I manage to squint my eyes open enough to see his bloodshot ones light with sick arousal at the sound of my pain. Every alarm bell is going off in my head, but my mind feels like a sea of tapioca, and I can't latch onto a thought long enough to get my body to obey my command to move.

136

I'm drowning. Sinking. Poe, please, help me!

The last thing I see before I pass out is the headlights from the car following us, reflecting through the rear-view mirror and illuminating my captor's cruel eyes, as silent screams echo through my soul, crying for help that will never come.

A shoulder digs painfully into my stomach as I'm carried and then dropped onto something soft that smells of mothballs and rot.

Ugh. Gross. Why does everything smell so bad?

I'm so horribly tired.

Somebody screams in pain, and I just want her to stop. Something sharp tears into the delicate pale skin on the underside of my arm. Liquid fire burns up my thigh, picking and pricking and jabbing. More tearing, and another guttural scream.

Shut up, already!

Hot breath and the stink of a ripe, unwashed body. Hands. So many hands. Ripping and pulling. Searing pain in my chest. The sounds of metal on metal slicing through the air.

Snick snick snick.

A trail of warmth slides down my leg.

I miss my mom. But why won't she stop screaming?

At last, the smooth, cold arms of unyielding darkness embrace me.

Why is my hair loose? Didn't I have it up when I left my aunt's?

The thick strands stick to the sides of my neck and face like cobwebs. The cloying smell of dead things makes me choke and gag. Rolling onto my side, I dry-heave a couple of times and almost blackout at the pain the movement jolts through my body. Lifting my arm makes the skin feel two sizes too small and like it might split apart, but I manage to convince my hand to wipe away the hair sticking to the sheen of sweat coating my forehead.

Slowly opening my eyes, I squint at the weak light filtering in through the cracked and dirty window high in the wall to my right.

Where am I?

Struggling to sit up, my breathing turns harsh and shallow, and dark splotches strobe through my vision as all the pain flares to life at once. Clenching my teeth against the high-pitched whine building in my throat, I struggle to control my racing heart as I take in my dilapidated surroundings. It looks like I'm in some kind of an old barn.

Old barn? Where would there be an old barn in Folkestone? Dammit it, Stella! Think!

Feeling something brush softly against my hand that's planted for balance on the torn and stained mattress beneath me, I look down, and for a minute, my brain refuses to register what my eyes show me. Reaching up with my free hand, I hear a rhythmic keening noise floating through the air, and it takes me a few seconds to associate the awful sound with my own voice.

It takes a few more seconds for me to realize that the hair stuck to my face and neck is no longer attached to my scalp.

Skimming my shaking fingers over my head, I can feel my long, raven hair is now a ragged mess. Hacked off in chunks just past my jawline, I'm sitting in the middle of the shorn pieces, like an abandoned baby bird in a broken nest.

Operating purely on instinct and driven by fear, I scan the floor around me and see what looks like a cell phone about ten feet away, butted up against the wall. With my skin, my nerves, and my guts shrieking the entire time, I manage to belly crawl off the mattress and through layers of unknown filth to grab it. Turning the phone over in my hand, I recognize it as mine, even with the new spidered cracks on the screen.

"Oh, God, please. Please," I beg to the empty room around me, my voice hoarse and stripped. Finding the power button, I hold it down and start to cry when the screen flashes to life. Flipping to the Find My app, I quickly share my location with Sunday's phone and open a new text message. My brain is having a hard time staying coherent, so I only type what I can manage.

HELP. PLEASE COME.

My arm falls to my side, the shattered phone sliding free as I sit pressed to the wall, slowly rocking back and forth.

Time doesn't exist as I fade in and out of consciousness. Memories bob to the surface and pop like oil-slicked bubbles. Trying to focus on the small window in the opposite wall, I suddenly remember I've always hated this particular shade of light. An awful rusty gold color that's reminiscent of old kitchen appliances. Cold sweat starts to form on the back of my neck, and my vision tunnels. Watching the light creep toward the clumps of my dark hair strewn across the stained mattress on the floor, I feel something trying to break free as my mind folds inward and down into the black hole I fall.

His voice booms through the tiny A-frame house, calling my name like thunder. Knowing that ignoring him won't make it stop and will only make him madder, I advance into the room with stilted steps, the mid-August heat turning my mother's bedroom into a hot box rank with the smell of sweat and fear. Tiny dust motes float through the dirty rays, dancing before my eyes in an awkward ballet that pulls my focus.

My mother, herself, is off doing motherly things, grocery shopping after getting her hair highlighted at the salon down on the corner. The man on her bed is alone and clad in only a velour bathrobe, the color of day-old burnt coffee with amber edges. From the corner of my twelve-year-old eye, I see him motion me closer impatiently, but my focus remains on those specks of dust still playing in the dying evening light from the west-facing windows.

The air conditioning unit in her room broke weeks ago, and the small fan humming feebly in the corner does nothing to move the fetid air. The man slides to the edge of the bed and reaches for my thin wrist, finally tired of waiting. In doing so, his robe falls open slightly, and I see he isn't wearing any underwear; the horrible thing between his legs left to bob and weave freely in its excitement. Terror rises quickly in my throat, and I can taste the grape Kool-Aid I drank at lunch.

The front door slams as my mother returns home from her errands, and he quickly reaches to tie his robe, letting me slip easily from his grasp. Turning, I creep silently to my bedroom, another crack forming in my fragile psyche. Too horrified to cry, I lay dry-eyed and motionless on my bed, listening to the sounds of the rats scratching in the walls.

Strong arms reach down and lift me effortlessly off the hard ground, and the sound of someone sobbing uncontrollably lures me back to the present. I stiffen and start to thrash, pushing feebly against the chest holding me until I hear Payne's voice as he grips me tighter.

"Stella, it's okay. You're safe, I promise. It's me. It's Payne. Shhhhhhh." He starts for the door, and I stare at the vein pulsing in his temple and the flex of his jaw as he turns back toward the sobbing. "Sun, take a few pictures of this fucking hellhole. We'll need them later. Grab her phone and anything else of hers those fuckers left behind." His golden-brown eyes shine with unshed tears as he glances quickly away from the remnants of my hair scattered in the dirt, and my heart squeezes painfully.

He carries me to Sunday's Range Rover as my friend comes running out of the abandoned barn, tears leaking from her reddened eyes and wiping her snotty nose on the sleeve of her sweater. Pulling open the rear passenger door, she climbs in and slides across the seat, motioning for Payne to load me in with her. He carefully lays me down with my head resting on Sunday's lap, before jogging around and sliding into the driver's seat. Gunning the engine, he deftly flips us about, a spray of gravel shooting up from the tires.

"I lost my shoe," I whisper. "I'm Cinderstella. Only, I didn't end up with a prince. I ended up with a monster."

"Stella, honey, you don't need a prince. You have us, and the monster will never touch you again."

Sunday's hand smooths what's left of my hair as her tears drip from her cheek onto mine, and Payne steers us toward home.

CHAPTER SIXTEEN

STELLA

*T*he bumpy back roads and twisting turns are making my stomach angry and my head pound. Even though somewhere in the recesses of my clouded brain I know the Rover is practically new and still has that new car smell, the stink of rot and fear is stuck in my nose and keeps making me gag. Throwing up right now seems like it would be extraordinarily painful and, well, just plain rude after they came to my rescue and all, so I grit my teeth against the bile and pray we get home soon.

Sunday lays her cold hand on my forehead and whispers comforting words and murmurs. Occasionally, her eyes meet Payne's in the rear-view, and it's like they can communicate telepathically or something. Like they operate on the same wavelength.

Or it's the drugs talking, and I'm hallucinating like a son of a bitch.

That makes me giggle for some reason, and I realize my mind is slowly clearing. The downside to the drugs wearing off? My pain receptors are firing on all cylinders. With every bump Payne hits, they flare. I have no idea what part of me is injured or how, but my body feels like a roman candle of agony right now—a constant slow burn interspersed with shocking jolts of blinding hurt. I try to ask Sunday a few times if we're there yet, but the pain keeps swallowing my words.

My mind wanders, trying to distance itself from the torment my body is feeling, and all of a sudden I hope that they haven't told anybody else they had to come and save my sorry ass. The last person I want to see right now is Poe.

He's also the *only* person I want to see.

Stop it, Stella! Stop tormenting yourself with thoughts of a guy who doesn't give a shit.

His words on the stairwell at Roxy's party come floating back to me, carried on a breeze of sadness and longing and anger. With my eyes closed, I don't have to see Sunday's face and the heartbreaking sadness etched there. The grief that she's feeling for *me*. Tears prick at the corners of my eyes, and I tell myself they're from the pain inflicted on me rather than Poe's words, or Sunday's sadness, or me feeling sorry for myself.

We make the turn into Tweedvale's lazily winding driveway and slip through the imposing iron gates. If I were in better shape, I would probably be freaking out at the thought of Cecily seeing me like this, but right now, I can't seem to care. My body is on fire inside and out, and my head is heavy and dull.

Payne glides to a smooth stop, and before he can even cut the engine, the back passenger side door opens roughly, and Spry reaches in to lift me out of the backseat.

"Hi, Spry. Your hair is messy. Why is your hair messy?

Did you just get out of bed?" My voice is fuzzy, laced thickly with pain, and the last of whatever drug I ingested at Roxy's party.

"You can tease me all you want about my grooming habits later. How about for now you just stay quiet and save your strength, okay?" he answers, his voice gruff with worry. Carrying me through the front doors, he starts the climb up the stairs, Sunday and Payne following.

Cecily is in my bedroom, laying out pajamas and turning back the sheets on my bed. When she hears us coming, she starts busying herself further and refuses to look at me.

"Auntie," the word floats between us, quiet and soft. Finally looking at me, her distress and guilt are invisible weights hanging heavy around her shoulders. As she leans toward me and brushes a strand of hair from my face, it comes loose and sticks to her hand. It was just bad luck she picked that particular piece of hair, but she looks horrified and starts to sob. Payne steps up to Spry's side and takes my tired body from his arms so the older man can move to comfort Cecily.

"Sun, can you grab the clean clothes off the bed?" He carries me into my bathroom and carefully sits me on the edge of the oversized tub, one hand on my back until he's sure I won't topple over. "You good here, New Girl?" I start to nod and wince when the world slips sideways for a second, my vision blurring.

"Yeah, I'm good." I croak, smiling at the nickname. He turns to leave, but I reach out and grab his arm. "Payne." My voice gets a little stronger with each word. "Thanks. You didn't have to come for me. So thank you."

"Stella, you're one of us." He says it so matter-of-factly. "We'll always come for you. Family is family." Seeing the tears well in my eyes, he lightens the mood as Sunday walks in with her arms full of pajama bottoms and T-shirts. "Plus, I think Sun might've cut off my junk if I didn't go with her when she got your message." He laughs at the eye roll she gives him.

"Like you even thought twice about it. You were as worried as I was." Dropping her cargo on the counter, she turns and steers Payne to the door. "Out. Go keep Miss B company. We have girl things to do."

Rubbing my eyes with the heels of my palms causes a stab of pain in my right eye, and I flinch.

"Fuck me, that hurt." With gentle fingers, I prod carefully around my eye socket, wondering if I'm going to have a shiner. Closing the bathroom door behind Payne, Sunday leans against the vanity, silvery hair in disarray, and dirt and tear stains streaking her face. For the first time since I met her, she appears to be at a loss for words. "Cat got your tongue, Easton?" I tease. Instead of the snappy comeback I'm expecting, she looks at me with sad eyes.

"Stell, don't ever do that to me again. To Cecily. To any of us." Crossing over to me, she sits beside me and wraps me in a gentle hug.

"Trust me, I don't plan on it." Her grip on me loosens just enough for me to pull back and see her face. "Sunday Grace Easton, thank you for coming to my rescue, and for everything you've done for me since I got here."

"You heard Payne. You're one of us. Family. And better than that, you're my best friend." Her hug this time is tighter, and my breath catches.

"You're my best friend too, weirdo. Now can you please help me take this shit off so I can get clean?" She nods hastily, and between the two of us, we manage to get me standing long enough to pull my ruined leather pants off, throwing them to the side along with my one remaining shoe.

The outside of my left thigh is already showing an ugly bruise and looks like it was nicked in a few spots by something sharp. It's hard to get a full picture, with it still caked in dried blood and dirt. To my relief, my panties are intact, though, and none of the pain I'm experiencing is between my legs.

So, rape wasn't the end goal. Thank God for that.

Sunday seems to be thinking along similar lines and raises her eyebrows questioningly. I shake my head, and she finally lets go of the breath I swear she's been holding ever since they found me in that barn.

I reach for my brush on the vanity and run it through what's left of my hair, strands falling around me like loose feathers. It took me forever to grow it out as long as it was, and it's the one thing I've always been vain about—rich and dark, shining blue-black in the light, like a raven's wing. Seeing it chopped like this brings tears to my eyes.

"Do you want me to try to fix it? I'm pretty good with stuff like that." Since she can't really make it any worse, I give her a half-hearted double thumbs up, and she goes in search of Cecily to ask for a pair of scissors.

For the next twenty minutes, I am entirely at the mercy of my well-meaning friend, internally resigned to having to find a hairdresser tomorrow.

"Okay, Bradleigh. Behold the magic of Sunday Grace."

Stepping in front of the mirror, I pause for a few beats before looking up and gasping in shock. What was quite literally a hatchet job is now a cute reverse bob, shorter in the back where the most significant chunks had been hacked off and angling smoothly to just past my chin in the front.

"Where in the hell did you learn to cut hair?" I ask in shock, tickled by what a great job she did. "This looks almost professional." Sunday blushes slightly before answering.

"It's no big deal. Just something I picked up when I was younger." She's visibly uncomfortable with my question and busies herself with dusting all the little loose hairs from my shoulders. It's her way of asking me to leave it alone without actually saying the words.

"You okay, Sun?"

"Yeah, I'm fine." She's not. I can see that she's not. "I'm going to run downstairs and get something to clean this hair up. Why don't you shower?" Her smile feels a little hollow, but after everything that's happened in the past twenty-four hours, I decide not to push it.

"Well, thanks for saving me a trip to the salon, bestie." Nodding, she leaves as I turn on the shower. Stripping off the last of my clothes, I yelp sharply when the thin fabric of my shirt rips away from my breast and the inside of my arm.

What the hell?

Examining the soft white flesh of my bicep, I find a patch of raw, bloody red skin surrounded by what looks like teeth marks.

Teeth marks?

Prodding gently, I can feel the deep bruise not yet visible. Moving to my breast, the same marks and underlying bruises cover a small area beside my nipple, some of the dried blood now ripped away and the skin underneath tender. A frenzied need to see if there are any others has me standing in front of the full-length mirror with my hands moving quickly over my naked skin. I feel for sore spots while my eyes search for similar injuries and find two more.

One is high on the inside of my right thigh, deeper than the others, and already a dark blue-black at the edges. The other is on the outside of my right hip near the row of small cuts, where it looks like somebody tried to cut away my pants and caught the skin at the same time.

That fucker gnawed on me like a goddamn chicken leg!

Anger is replacing the soul-numbing fear that engulfed me in that disintegrating barn. Being afraid makes me useless, unable to get my head above water. Anger, though, I can use. Anger gives me the strength to get through this. To go after the asshole who decided I was something to be used as a chew toy and thrown away like a piece of garbage.

When I step under the shower spray, the warm water stings when it hits certain spots and makes me hiss with pain, but it also feels like heaven, washing away the blood and dirt and stink.

Payne's lounging in my wingback chair, his socked feet propped up on the matching ottoman and a giant bowl of buttery popcorn in his lap, while Sunday stretches out on my bed with me. Neither one of them seemed to want to leave, and Cecily had no problem with it, so we're camped out in my room watching Hudson and Hicks back up Ripley on an alien planet.

I see Sunday's eyes slide quickly to Payne to gauge the degree of his attention on us. Happily munching on popcorn with his eyes glued to the television hanging at the foot of my bed, he doesn't seem to be paying any attention to us at all.

"We didn't tell him," she says quietly. "We didn't tell Poe what happened. When Raff told us what happened when he ran into you, we thought we'd just give you a little space. But then the girls and I tried to find you later, and you were gone." She sniffles, and I can tell she's trying to get through what she has to say without falling apart. "We went back and found Payne, Raff, and Heller, and they helped us look, but none of us could find you anywhere." She glances down, refusing to meet my eyes. "Poe left. After those awful things he said to you, he left with Hali."

Her revelation surprises me, but my gut-wrenching reaction to it doesn't.

"So, he doesn't know about any of this." It's a statement rather than a question. "He doesn't know I was drugged and left half-naked and abused in a broken-down barn." Another statement.

"Nobody knows except for Payne and me, and your aunt and Spry."

"Oh, thank God." My feeling of relief is snatched away as Sunday bursts my bubble.

"You have to tell him."

"Like hell I do! It's none of his business." I argue, incredulous at the suggestion.

"Yes, it is, Stell. It's bigger than just you. I'm sorry, but he needs to know." She looks at me with pleading eyes. "Please tell him."

"Sunday, no. I don't want to. I can't even remember what happened. He already hates me, and I don't want to play his bullshit games anymore. If he laughs or says that it was my fault, or worse yet, looks at me with pity, I don't think I'll be able to handle it. I'll either punch him in the face or cry. Or maybe both." I angle my face down so she can't see my flush. "As much as he hates me, my stupid heart still feels something for him, and I don't know how to stop it. His opinion matters to me."

"You'll be fine, New Girl. You're the badass babe from New York, and you're an Heir. You're more than a match for Poe Halliday." I nearly jump out of my skin when Payne interjects out of the blue. "And for the record, Poe doesn't hate you." He shoves another handful of popcorn in his mouth and talks around it. "Far from it."

I snort, and Sunday laughs, though I'm not sure if she's laughing at the ridiculousness of Payne's statement or my response to it. He was obviously paying more attention to us than we realized. Deciding I need a minute alone, I gingerly push myself off the bed and grab the almost empty bowl from Payne's lap.

"Hey," he frowns, "where are you going with that?"

"I'm just going to get a drink. You hoovered up all the popcorn, so I might as well make some more while I'm down there." He purses his lips and blows me an air kiss while rubbing his stomach.

"See, Easton? That's how you do it. Always take care of the man in your life." He laughs and catches the pillow Sunday throws at him with ease, tucking it behind his back.

"Do you want me to come with you?" She's already halfway off the bed as she asks.

"No. I'm good. You stay here; I'll be right back." She looks like she might argue with me for a minute, but she lowers herself back down and watches me like a mother hen.

Babying the swollen ankle I twisted on Roxy's stairwell while Poe ripped out my heart and handed it to me, I leave the two of them and take the stairs down to the kitchen.

CHAPTER SEVENTEEN

STELLA

ost of the kitchen is dark and quiet; the soft under-cabinet lighting the only illumination in the large room. Grabbing a glass from the cupboard, my hand shakes as I fill it with water from the fridge dispenser and some of it sloshes onto the floor.

"Shit." Ripping a few paper towels from the roll in the pantry, I drop them on the small puddle and dry it with my foot, holding on to my glass like a lifeline. Remembering another late night mopping a floor with my foot, I don't even notice my aunt until she speaks.

"I'll get it." Cecily's voice emerges from the shadows gathered around the long table and makes me jump, spilling more water.

"Jesus Christ! Auntie, what the hell are you doing sitting in the dark?" I squawk.

"Sorry, I didn't mean to scare you." Coming over to where I'm standing, she reaches down and finishes drying the floor, grabbing the soggy mess of paper towels, and throwing it in the trash.

"It's okay. I can get it myself. No big deal."

Let me just wait for my adrenaline to stop pumping.

"No." The word is solid and definitive.

"No? No, what?" I ask, confused.

"No. You aren't going to do this by yourself. You've had to do way too much in your life by yourself. You aren't alone anymore." Her face flushes with embarrassment and guilt. "I'm sorry I let you down. I should have protected you." Angry tears start to flow down her pink cheeks. "This is my fault. It was selfish of me to bring you here. It would have been easy enough just to send you money and make sure you were taken care of from a distance." Swiping the tears away with the back of her hand, she stands a little straighter. "This will not happen again. We'll find you a nice condo wherever you want to go, and I'll make sure you have everything you need. You can get on with your life and try to forget this town even exists." She jerks in surprise at my sudden harsh jolt of laughter that quickly turns into a cough.

"You think I could leave here now?" I question when my throat clears. "No way."

"Stella, be reasonable, please. Look at what just happened to you!" Her face is set in stone, the severe downturn of her mouth carving a harsh and rigid shape on her usually sunny features.

"That's exactly why I can't leave—not knowing what happened or why? I can't let that go. Though I do have a suspicion as to *who*." The side of my upper lip curls momentarily in disgust.

And, boy, is he going to regret that decision.

"Look, Auntie, I've never really been a part of anything. Even with my mom, she kept us separate from everything and everyone. She got worried when people started to get too close, so she pushed them away. I'm slowly learning

154

there was a reason for that, and I need to know what it was." She tries to interrupt, but I silence her with a raise of my palm. "I know it's dangerous. Trust me, I've been warned. I know it probably won't be good when I get to the bottom of it. But I have to know." Tilting my head to the side slightly, a shy smile settles over my lips. "Besides, I have you now. And Sunday. And Payne and the others." Poe's vicious words from last night flash briefly through my mind, and I shove them back into the dark. "I don't want to leave. Please don't make me leave." An ache builds in my throat at the thought. My aunt reaches out for me, her face softening at the pleading note in my voice as she wraps me in a warm hug.

"I don't want you to go anywhere, but I'm scared for you. When you didn't come home last night, and nobody knew where you were..." she trails off, a sob choking her words briefly. "When nobody knew where you were, all I could think of was your mother. She broke my heart when she left without a word." Her eyes puffy from tears, but bright and direct, she delivers her decision. "If you're going to stay, I need you to be careful. Very careful. And we are going to lay down some ground rules. Agreed?" Some of the tension leaves my bruised body, and my heart swells with love for this woman I didn't know a week ago, who now feels like home to me.

"Agreed. Thank you, Auntie, for letting me stay. For everything."

"Get some sleep. We'll talk more tomorrow. I'll call the headmistress and let her know you'll be taking a few days off." Hugging me as tightly as she dares, knowing how sore I am, she releases me and turns to go back to her bedroom, but I stop her with a hand on her arm.

"I'm going back to school tomorrow." She faces me again, reaching out and laying her hand on the side of my face as I speak. "I'm going to find out what happened and make sure whoever did it knows they will never do it again." My words come out strong and matter of fact. Wariness and pride jockeying for position over her features, she finally nods once.

"Alright. But you are never to be alone, got it? You make sure one of your friends stays with you." Running her fingers softly over my new shorter hair, she smiles. "Sunday did a good job. It suits you."

Grinning in thanks, I grab my glass and head back upstairs, my promise of more popcorn forgotten. Sleep won out over snacks anyway since Payne is zonked out in the chair, one arm behind his head, the other across his chest. Lifting the soft throw blanket from the end of my bed, I carefully put it over him, and he mumbles quietly in his sleep. Crawling in under the covers of my big comfy bed beside Sunday, my movement makes her stir and wake up enough to ask if I'm okay. Murmuring my assent, I turn off the television and fall into a deep and dreamless sleep.

My alarm starts going off far too early. Refusing to open my eyes, I reach out blindly to shut it off, my flailing raising a groan from beside me. Keeping my eyes closed, I smile.

"Good morning to you, too."

"Why is school so early? Are they trying to make it as terrible as possible?" Rolling over, she buries her face in the pillows. "Don't they know I need my beauty sleep?" Her muffled complaints make me laugh.

"Yes, Sunday, they are purposely trying to make you as ugly as possible. It's a grand scheme devised by the average-looking people of the world to level the playing field." She lifts her face out of the pillow and props herself up on her elbows.

"Are you calling me better than average-looking?" Flashing a cat that ate the canary grin at me, she throws the covers off and stands up, raising on to her tiptoes and stretching toward the ceiling. "That's a reason to get out of bed. I can't hide this beauty from the world." Rolling my eyes and grinning, I groan at her goofiness as she does a chicken walk over to the closet and disappears inside. "Dude," she says, poking her head out around the door. "I'm borrowing a uniform so I don't have to go home before school, 'kay?"

"Help yourself. Go use the shower first."

I'm just going to lie here and think of all the ways I can pay Bingham Ramsey back while I wait.

"Hey, when did Payne leave?" I raise my voice so she can hear me while in the depths of my closet, looking at the blanket folded neatly and stacked with the pillow on the chair.

"No idea, I didn't even hear him. His car is still at his place since I picked him up there when we went to find you, so I guess he probably called somebody to come and get him and take him home."

The two of us manage to get ready in decent time, even when a tear or two manages to escape as I blow-dry my now much shorter hair in a fraction of the time I'm used to. Sunday stays quiet, and like the best friend she is, helps me straighten and style it without comment. By the time we're ready, I have to admit that while it's not something I would have ever done on my own, the new shorter style looks pretty good on me.

As we walk into the kitchen a few minutes later, our eyes swing to each other, and our laughter is uncontrollable.

Payne is wearing what has to be one of Cecily's aprons judging by the frilled edging, a streak of flour on his handsome cheek as he cheerily hums a wordless tune and pours pancake batter onto the flat grill of the gas cooktop. My aunt sits at the island in front of one of three places set for breakfast, drinking her coffee and watching him over the rim of her cup with amusement.

"Ladies!" He exclaims when he sees us in the doorway. "Welcome to Pancake Heaven! Please have a seat." He gestures to the remaining two spots at the island, dripping batter from the ladle in his hand onto the floor. We slide into the seats next to Cecily and raise our eyebrows at her in question.

"Don't look at me; this was all his idea." She chuckles. Sipping the orange juice set out for us, Sunday and I watch Payne flip the pancakes once with an admirable level of skill, letting them finish cooking for a few minutes while he pulls a full stack out of the warming oven. Adding the new ones to the pile, he shuts off the oven and the cooktop and starts arranging food on plates with his back to us.

"Today, we have chocolate chip pancakes, with strawberries and bananas for the young ladies," he proclaims in a terrible fake accent, "and plain with blueberries for the mistress of the house." Setting our plates in front of us with a flourish, he sets to cleaning up.

My stack is topped with sliced bananas for eyes, and extra chocolate chips arranged in a smile. Leaning over to Sunday's, hers has the same chocolaty smile, but instead of banana slices, hers has strawberry halves for eyes that look a little too heart-shaped to be coincidental. She won't look at me, instead keeping her head down and trying to hide her pleased smile.

"Payne, if all of your food is like this, you are welcome to come and cook here anytime you'd like." Cecily makes an appreciative noise, her mouth full. "These are fantastic." Sunday and I both dig in and echo her sentiments wholeheartedly.

"Alas, ladies, I must leave you and go home to get ready for school." Glancing at his phone as it dings with a text message, he removes his apron and folds it neatly on the counter. "Thank you for letting me stay last night, Miss Bradleigh, and for letting me use the kitchen this morning." He starts backing out of the kitchen. "Sun, New Girl, I'll see you guys at school." Saluting, he turns and disappears down the hall to the front door.

Dropping my fork on my plate and wiping the syrup from my lips quickly, I tell my breakfast companions I'll be right back, and slide off my bar stool. I manage to catch up with Payne on the front porch, just as the Uber he ordered pulls up to the front steps.

"Thank you, Payne. For yesterday, for smiley pancakes this morning, for everything." I instinctively wrap my arms around him in a sisterly hug. "You're an excellent friend and a really great guy." He chuckles and hugs me back.

"Don't tell anybody. You'll ruin my street cred." He pulls back and winks. Glancing thoughtfully back at the house, he gets serious for a second. "Except that one inside. You can tell *her* what a nice guy I am." Running his hand through his hair, he shoots me a wistful grin and jogs down the stairs, slipping into the back of the waiting car and waving once before it drives off.

"Oh, I think she knows *exactly* what kind of guy you are, Payne Emerson, even if she won't admit it," I say with certainty to the fresh morning breeze before heading back inside to finish breakfast.

CHAPTER EIGHTEEN

POE

*M*y head is pounding, and my legs feel like wet cardboard. The arm curled under my cheek is asleep to the point of not feeling attached at all anymore. But for thirty blissful seconds, the only sensations I experience are the discomfort of sleeping in a fucked-up position and a decent hangover before it all comes flooding back.

The words I spit at the girl who unknowingly has my heart.

The devastated look on her beautiful face.

The soul-ravaging shame at being the cause of her humiliation and pain.

Dragging the back of my hand across my dry lips, I blink bits of sandy grit out of my eyes.

I have to fix what I broke. Or at least try to.

Getting myself vertical is more challenging than I expected. Once I'm there, my headache makes its presence fully known, a dull, throbbing helmet, and my thankfully empty stomach clenches and unclenches a few times, undecided if it wants to turn inside out or not.

Jesus, how much did I drink last night?

Scanning the sand around my makeshift bed, I count the empties as I grab them, a little surprised to realize that I finished off eight here, along with the two at the party. I shove them back in the cases and stow them in the trunk before going in search of my boots, taking the water bottle I keep in my gym bag with me.

Gravity is so not my friend right now, and she makes me take a seat and a few deep breaths. While I'm trying to get my shit together enough to go home and fall into my bed, I check my phone and see texts from Payne, Raff, and Sunday. Raff's and Payne's are of the pretty standard variety, just checking to make sure I'm okay, but Sunday's... Well, Sunday's is something entirely different.

I KNOW YOU'RE AN ASS SOMETIMES, BUT I NEVER TOOK YOU FOR CRUEL. HOW COULD YOU DO THAT TO HER? I'M SO DISAPPOINTED IN YOU.

That one hurts. Sunday is like my sister, and her opinion is important to me. Having her say she's disappointed in me is so much worse than her telling me to fuck off or calling me an asshole.

Don't worry, Sun, I'm right there with you. Nobody could be more disappointed in me than me right now.

Deciding to leave it be, for now, I shuffle my sorry ass back to my car and head home, my ruin of the only girl I've ever really wanted playing on a loop in my head.

After sleeping like the dead for most of the day, I wake up feeling marginally more human, and a whole lot more upset by the shitty choice I made last night. I drag myself into the shower and stand under the hot, full blast spray, letting it burn my skin as some perverse form of penance.

Though it does nothing to erase the fact that I'm a prick of epic proportions, at least it clears some of the hangover-fog from my head. Wrapping a towel around my hips, I step out and swipe my hand across the mirror, leaving a clear streak in the condensation. Not liking the face staring back at me very much right now, I look away quickly and grab my toothbrush to scrub the taste of stale beer out of my mouth.

A sharp knock on my bathroom door startles me mid-brush, and I jab myself in the gums.

Shit, that hurt.

"Yeah?" I ask, spitting a mouthful of bloody toothpaste into the sink.

"Poe. Downstairs in five, son."

Dad? He's not due home for another month.

"Okay, be right down!" I answer and hear him close my bedroom door as he leaves.

Throwing on gray joggers and a faded black shirt, I run my hands through my wet hair and take the stairs to the sunroom my dad has liked to use as the forum for his talks with me since forever. Surprisingly, my mother perches on the edge of the long white couch. Her back ramrod straight, she looks like she wants nothing more than to drive something sharp through the back of my father's head as he stands staring out the floor-to-ceiling and wall-to-wall windows. The thinly veiled hate in her expression gives me chills.

"You're home early, sir." He turns at the sound of my voice and motions me over next to him, reaching to shake my hand with his typical firm grip.

"How are you, Poe? I hear there's been some excitement

lately." Shifting his eyes toward my mother for a brief minute, she flinches under his gaze and looks away.

Okay, something fucked up is going on. She never yields to him. Never. Not in front of me.

"Excitement? I'm not sure I understand." Moving to the wet bar in the corner, he pours himself a Macallan, neat, swirling it gently and notably not offering my mother anything.

"The Bradleigh Heir is home now." A statement, not a question, and a knife in my gut. "She looks quite a bit like her mother, I'm told." *My* mother is turning seven shades of barely contained rage, still sitting on the couch like she's Velcroed to it.

"I don't know what her mother looked like, but Stella is beautiful."

"Stella, is it?" Smiling softly, he nods in approval. Handing me his rocks glass, he holds up a finger and leaves the room. I'm so damn confused, I mindlessly take a sip of the scotch and enjoy the smooth heat the amber liquid leaves as I swallow. I try to hand the glass back to him with an apology when he returns, but he waves it away.

"Drink it. A little hair of the dog." He winks knowingly, handing me the photo in his hand before moving to the bar and pouring himself a fresh drink. Shrugging, I take another sip and look down at the picture.

A group of teenagers around my age is lounging on the front steps of Woodington. I recognize the much younger version of my father, along with Payne's, Heller's, Sunday's, and Aylie's dads, and Raff's and Roxy's moms. The eighth person in the group, the one leaning against Raff's mom and holding my dad's hand, could be Stella. Except for the color of her eyes, the resemblance is incredible. The wide smile that lights her entire face and long dark hair stands out like an orchid in a room full of roses. Shocked, I look up and find my father staring at me, a sad smile on his lips.

"Catherine. That was taken seven months before she disappeared."

I almost forgot my mother was even in the room until she launches off the couch with a howl and grabs for the photo, her long red nails clicking together like lobster claws.

"EUNICE. SIT. DOWN. NOW." My father bellows before she can rip the image from my hand, and with a feral whine, she turns on him, spewing her filth.

"You're still carrying a torch for that whore, aren't you, Holt? After all these years, it's her perfect little cunt you lust after. I've never seen anybody as pussy-whipped as you were. As you still *are*." Her eyes wild, she spins and points at me. "It must be genetic, because now, your weak and pathetic excuse for a son is trying to stick his prick in her trash bag of a daughter. Well, I fixed it then, and I've fixed it now." Fluffing her hair like she didn't just go batshit crazy, she starts to walk away when my father blocks her path with his imposing six-foot-four frame.

"What do you mean you fixed it? Fixed what, Eunice?" The words are quiet but heavy with the threat of violence, packing more punch than anything I've ever heard him say. My mother's eyes widen in the face of my father's icy calm.

I have never seen him like this before. Beyond angry. Beyond furious. Usually, he's utterly dismissive when it comes to my mother and her drunken ranting.

Not this time.

This time he looks like he could actually beat her to death and bury her corpse in the yard without a second thought.

Having been asked by my father to leave the room last night before my mother offered any sort of explanation, I spent the night sleepless and confused.

My dad and Stella's mom? That's crazy. What the hell am I supposed to do with that information?

By the time my alarm goes off, I'm already showered, dressed, and trying to figure out how to apologize to Stella for my reprehensible behavior at the party. The house is eerily silent as I tiptoe into the kitchen, only to find my father already seated at the island, drinking coffee and reading a battered old paperback.

"Morning, Dad." My voice is hushed, something about the silence of the house demanding it.

"Good morning, son." Taking off his reading glasses, his eyes—the same shade of deep blue as mine—are bloodshot and red-rimmed.

"You okay?" I down a glass of grapefruit juice, making him wince and chuckle at my choice of breakfast drink.

"Still have no idea how you drink that stuff. Tastes like paint thinner and feet."

"Exactly how many feet dipped in paint thinner have you tasted, Dad? Is this some kind of kinky thing I don't want to know about?" Laughing, I give him a mock suspicious face and sit down beside him after depositing my empty glass in the dishwasher.

"If only that were the extent of my problems right now. The extent of *our* problems." He sighs heavily, looking older than I've ever seen him look, and scaring me a little. My father has always been larger than life. Strong. Confident. The man sitting beside me this morning seems like a worn out and sad caricature of himself.

"What happened with Mother last night?" The question has to be asked, though I'm not sure I want to hear the answer.

"I'm still sorting a few things out, son, but I promise I'll tell you everything soon, okay?" He scrubs his hand through his dark hair that's only recently started graying at the temples. "For now, just know that a long time ago, I loved a girl with everything I was. From the time we were small, we knew we were meant to be together."

He pauses, momentarily adrift in the sea of memories.

"When she disappeared, my heart broke. *I* broke. I was inconsolable for the first six months. The next six I spent trying to drown my memories of her in every piece of ass and bottle of booze I could find. Finally, I had to accept she wasn't coming back, and your grandparents started pushing me toward Eunice. She wasn't their first choice—or even their eighth—but her family had a business connection your grandfather was desperate to have, and she was more than willing. It didn't matter to her that I didn't even really like her, let alone love her. She wanted the elevation in status that went along with the Halliday name." He grimaces. "I've never stopped loving Catherine, even when she stopped loving me."

The air around us is heavy with sadness and regret.

"I'm sorry, Dad." My words are soft but full of sincerity. Seeing my father hurting is something I've never seen before, and it's hard for me to watch. Closing his book, he hands it to me.

"Take this. I've had it since I was younger than you are now. It's gotten me through a lot." He grabs me by the shoulder and pulls me in for a quick hug. "Find Stella and make sure she's alright. Apologize for whatever happened between you two and fix it, for the sake of both your futures. Don't let anybody keep you apart from her. We need to make arrangements to have Stella formally introduced to the families as the Bradleigh Heir as soon as possible."

Our futures? And how the hell does he know something happened between Stella and me? What am I missing?

"Dad, what the fuck is going on?" Not one to swear in front of my father, I expect some kind of a reaction from him, some sort of reprimand for my foul language, but he just shakes his head.

"Go to school, Poe. We'll talk later. Go find your girl." With that, he leaves me alone in the empty kitchen, clutching a worn copy of *The Collected Works of Edgar Allan Poe* and wondering if this was the end of the nightmare or only the beginning.

Raff and Heller are waiting for me outside the main doors when I pull up.

"Where'd you go Saturday night?" Raff's concern is evident, but so is something else, something he doesn't want to ask.

"Had to bail. Couldn't deal with the bullshit."

"Did you, uh, leave alone?" Heller shoves him and speaks up.

"For fuck's sake, stop being a big pussy, Essex." Leveling his gaze directly at me, he point-blanks it for me. "Somebody saw you leave with Hali. At least somebody saw *you* leave, with her tagging along behind you in her hoochie dress, and neither one of you came back. So, two and two, you know?" He runs his hand through his blond hair, looking uncomfortable.

Jesus Christ, what the hell is going on around here? Can this day get any fucking weirder?

"No. And no. Oh, and by the way, no. Do you think I'm insane? Give me some credit. She followed me out to my car, looking to get a piece, and I told her to fuck off. Again. I left her in Roxy's driveway." Yanking open the front doors, we start down the hall toward my locker. "Did you guys honestly think I left to go fuck Hali?" The thought alone brings a little bit of my grapefruit juice back up.

"Nah, not really, but it looked a little strange. And then when nobody heard from you all day yesterday, we figured maybe you were doing the ultimate walk of shame." That makes me laugh for some reason, but I nearly choke on it when I see Stella and Sunday up ahead at their lockers.

She cut off all her hair! When the hell did she do that? Why did she do that? And how is it possible that she looks even hotter?

"Holy shit! New Girl looks smokin' with shorter hair!" Raff's eyes nearly bug out of his head, and he looks around quickly to see if anybody else heard him. "I said that out loud—*really* loud—didn't I?"

"Sure did. Smooth, Raff, real smooth." Grinning at his embarrassment, I slap him on the back and walk toward the hallway that takes me the long way to my locker, looping around the ones assigned to the girls. "I'm going this way, you coming?" Heller comes with me, but Raff walks straight to Stella, picking her up and twirling her around.

"He does love the ladies, doesn't he?" Heller smirks as we walk away.

"And the ladies love him right back." With a last glance back at the three of them standing and laughing together, I watch Stella stand on her tiptoes and kiss Raff's cheek. Sighing, I fold my heart up in a little box, tucking it away just to get through the day.

CHAPTER NINETEEN

STELLA

We pull into the school parking lot thirty minutes before our first class, after a nearly silent drive that was heavy with anticipation. Turning off the Rover's engine, Sunday sits facing straight ahead, her fingers clenched around the steering wheel.

"How do I get through this day without throat punching somebody?" she asks, still not looking at me.

"First we have to figure out for sure who deserves the throat punching. The obvious culprit just doesn't strike me as clever enough to pull this off on his own. After that, I'm fully okay with setting you loose on them, but only after I get my turn."

You have no idea the shitstorm about to rain down on you, Bingham fucking Ramsey.

Taking a few exaggerated deep breaths, she finally turns to face me, and I see my need for payback reflected back at me. With a quick *'wonder twin powers, activate!'* fist bump, we leave the quiet of the Rover and walk into the belly of the beast.

The first thing I notice is the stares my new look is

getting. The second thing is that people are no longer respectfully moving to the side for Sunday to pass while she drags the new girl along behind her; they are moving for me now as well.

Okay, this is weird.

We're almost at our lockers when I'm abruptly lifted from behind and twirled around before being set back down and crushed against a firm chest.

"I forgive you for telling me to fuck off, New Girl. Tell me you still love me!" Raff's voice rumbles with affection. Hugging him back, I stand on my tiptoes and kiss his cheek.

"I'm sorry, Raff," I whisper so only he can hear. Letting me go and stepping back, I get the full force of his dancing green eyes and cheerful smile.

"Awww, like I said, I forgive you. Where'd you disappear to, though? We looked but couldn't find you anywhere." I'm saved from having to answer as Payne sidles up to us and claps his friend on the back.

"Morning, shithead." He teases with a big grin. "Good morning, lovely ladies, how was the rest of your weekend?" He really is the best guy, and I could kiss him for what he's doing, pretending he hasn't seen us since Saturday night.

"'Morning, shithead'? How come they get the nicey-nice, and I get 'morning, shithead'?" Raff asks with mock offense.

"Because they are far better looking than you are, and you *are* a shithead." Putting his friend in a headlock, they tussle their way down the hall to class, leaving Sunday and I laughing and shaking our heads.

The morning passes slowly, and the closer we get to lunch, the more restless I get. Bingham is AWOL so far, and I'm wondering if he'll show his weasely face at all. Tossing our books into our lockers, Sunday and I walk to the cafeteria, and Payne materializes seemingly out of thin air and is suddenly walking on my other side.

My two saviors making sure I'm okay.

I love them for it, but the main person they're going to need to check on is Bingham after I smash his face in.

Today I sit facing the room between Roxy and Payne, my back to the wall behind our table, and Sunday and Aylie across from us. From this vantage point, I see the exact moment Poe walks in, flanked by Heller and Raff.

The exact moment he sees me.

The exact moment confusion, desire, and shame all somehow find a home on his handsome face at the same time. Locking eyes with him, I blink slowly once and look away, effectively dismissing him. I feel his anger and hurt flare as he takes his usual spot at the opposite end of the table.

You may not be at the top of my shit list right now, dickhead, but you're still on it. Let's see how much you enjoy being ignored.

Heller reaches across the table and ruffles my hair as he sits down next to Aylie.

"Nice lid, New Girl. Looks hot."

"Thanks, Surfer Boy." I take a bite of my salad, talking around it. "Still have bigger balls than you do." He snorts loudly, and Sunday reaches across the table to high five me. After giving him a playful wink, I try to focus back on eating my lunch, but I can feel the weight of Poe's eyes on me constantly, and under the table, my leg starts to do that nervous shake like it did on the plane.

The room around me swirls with conversations, shrieks, and laughter, and I let it flow around me until my ears pick out one voice that brings every nerve ending in my body to attention.

Bingham Ramsey.

My head snaps up, and my face hardens as my eyes rapidly seek him out.

There you are, you sadistic, plastic motherfucker.

Payne feels the shift in my posture, and his questioning gaze follows mine. As soon as he sees the object of my focus, he starts to push away from the table, expression cold and his body coiled tight. Sunday, realizing almost too late what's happening, kicks me under the table to break my trance and shakes her head ever so slightly with her mouth set in a tight line. My pinhole vision widens back to normal, and I reach for the loyal and protective boy beside me, latching onto his arm before he can entirely leave his chair.

"Payne," I murmur under my breath, forcing him to lean into me so that he can hear what I'm saying. "Please don't. I appreciate it, but this is my fight." His eyes search my face, looking for truth. "Please." The taut muscles in his forearm relax under my hand, and I know he's wordlessly agreed. He plants a chaste kiss on the side of my head and pulls back up to the table, shooting Sunday a small, closed-lip smile before turning his attention back to his lunch. Looking back to where Bingham was, all I see now are bubble-headed rich girls making eyes at the rest of the football team.

Dammit. Where'd he go?

My eyes pass over Poe in my quick visual sweep of the cafeteria and are immediately drawn back to him when I notice the raw emotion swirling in his eyes.

He knows something's up. He can feel the tension coming from this end of the table, but he doesn't know why. All he knows is his boy is pissed, and that it has something to do with me.

Under the weight of his stare, my lungs suddenly feel like two lead balloons in my chest, and I need to get out of here and catch my breath.

"I need some air," I mutter. "I'll see you guys in a bit." Breaking my promise to Cecily about not being alone, I slide my chair back and stride out of the room before anybody has time to say anything to stop me. Once in the hallway, I spot Hali walking toward the courtyard doors cackling and squealing with her bitchy friends, so I choose the opposite direction and the student lounge instead. During lunch, it seems to be empty usually, so I'm hoping to sit for a minute and figure out some kind of a plan to neuter Malibu Ken without getting caught.

Staring in shock at the spectacle on the wall, tears of embarrassment and rage burn the back of my throat.

Fuck, no. I will not cry. Not here. I might puke, but I will not cry.

My nails dig bloody half-moons into the soft flesh of my palms, and my teeth clamp together hard enough to cause an instant tension headache. Everything in me twists, and the hollow, burning emptiness in my chest threatens to swallow me whole.

The bulletin board in the student lounge covers most of one wall. About five feet high and seven feet wide, its cork face is usually reserved for random event announcements and club sign-up sheets.

Not today, though.

Today, nearly every square inch of the stupid fucking thing is plastered in grossly enlarged photos of *me*. A half-naked and very messed up me. I have been trying unsuccessfully to dredge the events of Saturday night out of the dark, drug-induced fog surrounding them, but to no avail. Seeing them on display like this is a sharp knife splitting open the belly of a fish. The guts of it all come pouring out, and suddenly I'm back in that dank, dirty barn again.

My eyes flick over and back from one lewd and disturbing image to the next in quick succession, almost like my brain is trying to keep me from focusing on any single harrowing scene for too long.

Flick.

A close-up of my upper half, shirt pulled up and off one arm entirely, bloody teeth marks in the underside of my bicep.

Flick.

Drug-fogged violet eyes smeared with runny black, fear dripping down my face along with my tears.

Flick.

Heavy industrial-looking scissors, frozen in the seconds before they jaggedly bite through my beautiful dark hair.

Flick.

Legs splayed out, my leather pants a shredded ladder up one thigh, another bite mark visible through the holes, small cuts oozing into a single crimson thread and pooling beside me.

Flick.

Aggressive, meaty, masculine hands digging their way under my dirt-streaked waistband.

Wait.

Stop.

Go back.

Even though everything in me is screaming in revulsion, I move closer to the nightmare on display in front of me. Focusing on one of the images of my hair in particular, my eyes don't see the scissors at all anymore.

They see nothing but the hands.

I know those hands, just like I knew Bingham was too bland and stupid to think up this plan on his own.

The architect of this little scheme did a shitty job of hiding her identity. Right at the very edge of the image, I can make out just enough of the rose gold and emerald ring on her third finger. The heat of freshly kindled rage spreads within me, burying the shattered pieces of my heart, and fanning the flames of revenge.

"What the fuck?" Poe's soft exclamation of shock comes from about a foot behind me, his bag thudding to the floor as it slides off his shoulder, causing me to jump. Usually, I'm so attuned to his presence that he can't enter a room without me feeling it, but apparently, my Poe-dar is malfunctioning today, which sucks. I fucking hate being caught off guard, even on a good day, and this sure as hell wasn't a good day.

"Poe, please, just leave," I plead, not ready to have him witness my shame on display.

"Fuck that, Stella! What is all of this shit?" he demands, confusion and anger warring for dominance in his voice. Shoving me to the side to get a closer look at the scenes papering the board, he rakes a hand through his thick dark hair, making it stand up in messy spikes and whorls before spinning around to face me. The darkness swirling through his stare, coupled with the rigid set of his jaw, would probably scare somebody else. But not me. Matching his pissed-off glare with my own, I stand my ground.

"Just leave it alone, Poe," I snarl. "It doesn't concern you." Flipping him my middle finger, I turn to leave.

"DON'T YOU FUCKING MOVE!" he roars. Closing the distance between us in two long strides, he purposely grabs my upper arm right where the bruises from the bite mark are turning a lovely dark purple under my white button-down. "Let me see your arm."

"Ouch! You asshole! Let me go!" Trying to jerk my arm out of his steel grip hurts like hell, and I realize I'm at his mercy until he decides to release me. I hiss out an angry breath and look him straight in his stormy blue eyes. "What? You have something to say, Poe? Some pearls of rich boy wisdom for me?" With every biting word, I step a little closer until I'm nose to nose and toe to toe with him. "Or do you want to finish the conversation you started on the staircase at Roxy's?" He visibly flinches, a crack opening in his menacing façade.

"Cut the shit, Stella," he warns. "I want to know who the hell did this." Keeping hold of my injured arm, he reaches up with his free hand and gently wraps a strand of my now chin-length hair around his index finger. "Now I know what happened to your long hair." Seeing my lips press tightly together and my violet eyes darken even further, Poe leans down and whispers next to my ear. "Don't worry, it looks good. Sexy as hell." Letting go of my hair, he trails his finger softly along the underside of my jaw to my chin, which he holds tenderly between his thumb and forefinger. My breath quickens involuntarily as his beautiful mouth feathers over mine just once. Quietly, so quietly I'm not even sure I hear him correctly, he speaks his promise in three words. "They will pay."

With that, he lets go of my arm and steps back, grabbing his bag off the floor and stalking up to the images on the board. He pauses for a few seconds as if committing them all to memory, reaches up and rips one down, studying it carefully as if for confirmation. Swearing a blue streak under his breath before crumpling it in his fist, he turns to meet my gaze straight on. My heart pounds as he drops the mask and lets me see all of the desire, the pain, and the apologies hidden underneath, then turns and tosses the torn photo in the trash can next to the door on his way out. I hear Sunday's voice as he passes her outside the door on her way into the lounge.

"Poe? What's wrong?" After the past few days, I can't blame her for the fear coloring her voice.

"Go and take care of your girl, Sunday." He snarls and takes off down the hall.

"New Girl? You in here?" She pokes her head in and sees me standing stock-still, shocked by the real face he let me see. Did that just happen? Reaching up to touch my lips where his brushed only a minute ago, I feel my cheeks flush.

Poe Halliday's mood swings are going to give me a nasty case of whiplash.

"Stell! Earth to Stella!" Sunday laughs. "What happened between you two? Did he apologize? You guys finally admit you're hot for each other?" Reaching down, she grabs a piece of partially crumpled paper off the floor. Straightening up, she glances at the glossy image in her hand and then shoots me a big sassy grin.

Wait for it.

She pauses.

Her grin falters and falls slowly off her face as her brain registers what she just saw.

"Stell?" she asks soberly, a quiver creeping into her voice. I close my eyes briefly and take a deep breath, then jerk my chin toward the bulletin board she hasn't noticed yet. Sunday meets my gaze with uncertainty, then slowly turns her head in the direction of my nod. Her gasp is harsh and painful as she absorbs what's on display. The moment the awful reality of what happened to me the other night sinks in is palpable. When she finally turns back to me, her eyes are shining with tears. "Oh my God. I am going to fucking destroy Bingham Ramsey. I'm going to rip his fucking dick off and shove it straight up—" I cut her off and reach for her hand, pulling her to stand beside me. Together we stare at the remnants of that night in front of us.

"First off, no, you're not. That honor is all mine. But, Sun, it wasn't just him." I point out the photo of my hair about to be hacked off. "Look at the fingers." It takes about seven seconds for her to recognize the ring, and she squeezes my hand in hers hard enough to make me wince, vengeance lighting up her tawny eyes.

"Hali," she spits out the name like a mouthful of acid.

"Hali," I confirm. "Fucking Barbie is going down too."

CHAPTER TWENTY

Sunday and I are on our way out of the lounge when we hear the unmistakable sound of a body hitting a locker. Hard. We both start walking quickly toward the fight, the crowd parting smoothly to let us through.

The scene in front of me is straight out of a movie. Poe has Bingham up against the lockers, feet dangling two inches off the floor as he holds him there by his throat. Raff, Heller, and Payne form a half-circle behind Poe, almost begging one of the football players to try to step in and help their quarterback.

The tendons on the sides of Poe's neck stand out from the strain of holding Malibu Ken in his current position. His clenched jaw and dark, lowered brow convey just how badly he wants to pop the idiot's head off his neck like a human Pez dispenser. Bingham's face is turning an unattractive shade of mottled purple-red under his California tan.

"You are one sick fuck, Ramsey. How many other girls have you done this to? Or was Stella special?" Poe's eyes darken further, and the smirk that twitches across his lips is cold and threatening. "You knew you'd never get anywhere with her, that she'd see right through to your shitty, rotten core, so you decided to fucking drug her?"

A collective gasp runs through the crowd at that revelation, and Poe purposely loosens his grip for a split second, just to have the honor of smacking Malibu's head off the locker again. "I've had a really bad weekend, fuckface, and you just gave me the best reason in the world to take it all out on you. I will gladly fucking end you." His forearm tenses, the muscles rippling under his tattoo and making it appear alive. Payne turns away from crowd control and faces the shitweasel currently pissing his pants while hanging from Poe's fist.

"Ramsey, you may be a nasty fucker, but you are way too stupid to have done this all on your own. What I want to know, before Halliday here feeds you your own ass, is who else was in on it?" The creepy quiet voice is one I haven't heard from Payne before.

Malibu looks like he wants to say something, but is currently fighting for enough air just to breathe, so I step forward, Sunday backing me up.

"It was Hali. Her ring. It was her holding the scissors." Bingham's eyes look like they are going to pop out of their sockets at any second, but he still manages to slide them in my direction while trying to nod his head in confirmation. Poe doesn't glance my way at all, but I can see the muscles in his jaw flexing, and I know he heard me.

Shit. He's going to snap Bingham's neck. I need to stop this.

As pissed as I am at Poe, I care about him way too much to let him ruin his life for me. This was not how I thought it would play out when I came here to Folkestone to meet my mother's younger sister. Enrolling at Woodington, meeting the Heirs and learning I'm one of them myself, finding a place where I belong—none of that was on the agenda. And him. Poe Halliday was not something I expected, and despite his mood swings, and the awful things he's said to me, my heart tells me there's far more to our story. At this moment, the choice is mine to make.

"Poe." His name is soft as it crosses my lips. His jaw twitches again, but he still won't look at me. Sunday nudges me, and I step forward, slipping my right hand into his left as it clenches and unclenches by his side, ready to start throwing punches. The electricity between us picks up again, little tingles running up my arm. Not releasing the chokehold on Malibu, he turns his head toward me, the fire in his eyes tempered by the faintest glimmer of hope.

"Star?" he murmurs, so that only can I hear him. My hand tightens around his.

"Come on, let's get out of here. Take me for a drive so we can talk, okay?" I keep my voice light and coaxing, but firm. Not taking his eyes away from my face, he slowly lowers Bingham until his feet are on solid ground again and relaxes his grip around his throat slightly. Of course, Bingham being the stupid ass he is, decides this is a good time to start talking shit.

"What the hell, Halliday? You take orders from your bitch now? Pussy." His laugh sounds just like the jackass he is. "Speaking of pussy, hers was real ni—" Not giving Poe time to react, I step in between them, right up in Malibu's face.

I am so very over this shit.

"You really are dumber than a box of fucking rocks, aren't you, Bingham?" I ask, the level of his stupidity blowing my mind. "You have no idea how nice my pussy is, and you never will, you lying sack of shit," I state. "What the fuck kind of name is *Bingham* anyway? Were your parents just hoping you'd get your ass kicked on the regular?" His pretty-but-bland face twists like he's got something to say, but I've had enough, and I raise my voice for the crowd to hear. "By tomorrow morning, the Heirs will make sure the fathers of every teenage girl in Folkestone find out that you like to drug unsuspecting females." He pales noticeably, and I feel Sunday take a step closer to me as Roxy and Aylie move out of the crowd to join us. "I'd be trying to find a place to hide, fuckwad, because those daddies will stop at nothing to protect their little girls from a rapist-in-training like you."

There is silence all around us as Bingham looks like he's going to choke on his tongue.

"If you ever even think about pulling that shit again, it won't be Poe coming after you; it'll be me. By the time I'm done with you, you'll be pissing sitting down for the rest of your pathetic life."

Released from Poe's brutal grip and stinging from my threats, Bingham scurries off like a cockroach in the revealing light of day.

The eight of us are gathered in the parking lot, having decided as a group to skip the last two classes of the afternoon.

Now that the rest of them know what happened to me on Saturday night, I'm strangely relieved. I was sure all I would feel from them would be pity and blame once they found out, but that couldn't be further from the truth. All I feel is their strength, support, and pride.

"New Girl, you are *bad*ass. I could disappear that fucker

and Hali both for what they did, but the way you handled yourself in there was awesome." Raff wraps me in a giant hug, his face beaming like a proud daddy. "I'm not sure who Ramsey was more afraid of, you or Poe."

"My money's on her," Heller interjects from his spot leaning against Sunday's Rover, his arm loosely around Roxy's shoulders. "He was pissing his pants at the threat of physical violence from Halliday, but when New Girl here threatened him, he turned white as hell and nearly shit himself." From her spot cross-legged on the hood of her car, Sunday coughs anything but delicately, making us all laugh as we turn our attention to her.

"So, threatening him with the Heirs, huh?" she asks. "Does that mean you're staying? That you're a part of us?" The hopeful note in her voice is something she can't entirely hide, and something that makes me smile indulgently.

"Yeah, if my aunt is okay with it, I'd like to stay." I tap my lip thoughtfully. "I wonder if anybody around here is in the market for a permanent pain in the ass best friend with a little New York flavor?" With a happy scream, she scrambles off the hood and launches herself at me.

"You're hired!" Hugging me tightly, she sniffles a few times and whispers in my ear. "I'm so proud of you, Stell, for standing up to that asshole, and I'm so happy you want to stay." Suddenly, Roxy and Aylie fling themselves at us too, and we're a knot of four laughing, weepy girls all hugging each other. The guys give us a few minutes before Payne clears his throat.

"Hey, Sun, we have that thing this afternoon, remember? We should probably get going." Sunday looks over at him like he's lost his mind until his raised eyebrow and subtle head tilt toward Poe clue her in.

"Right! That was today, wasn't it? That thing. Almost forgot about that." She coughs. "Uh, Poe, Stella came with me today. Can you give her a ride home?" Grinning and rolling his eyes at her utter lack of subtlety, he nods.

"I think I can manage that." He looks directly at me, a hint of challenge flaring in his expression. "You okay with that plan, Star?"

"Sure. Sounds good." My cheeks heat at the public use of his intimate nickname for me. With a last squeeze, Sunday tells me she'll call me later, and her and the girls pile into the Rover, waving as they pull away.

"Welcome to the family, New Girl." Raff gives me one of his blinding smiles and plants a kiss on the top of my head before joining Payne and Heller, walking off in the direction of their cars, and leaving Poe and me alone. He slides smoothly to his right and opens the passenger door.

"You still want to go for that drive? Or I can just take you home if you'd rather do that." His hesitancy is endearing. Like he's afraid I'm going to tell him to go fuck himself and disappear in a puff of smoke.

Straight-faced, I sidle up beside him and slip into the passenger seat without a word. He makes an appreciative sound low in his throat and closes the door for me before coming around the other side and getting behind the wheel.

"I'm sorry, Star." Without starting the engine, he puts both hands on the wheel and keeps his head down as he talks. "Those things I said, I didn't mean…" He falters.

"I know."

"When I said this thing between us, whatever it is, is dangerous…"

"I know."

"You know? What do you know?" Frustrated by my calm, two-word answers, he finally turns to look at me.

"Before we go anywhere, I need to make sure you understand. From the minute you literally ran into me at the airport, I haven't been able to think clearly. You drive me nuts—your secret smiles, the way you throw your head back when you laugh, your fierce and unbreakable spirit. Everything in you speaks directly to everything in me. I fought it because it scares the shit out of me, but it's like I need you near me to be able to breathe." The look on his face is so naked and open, his eyes showing me I could crush him in an instant and begging me not to. "I pushed you away and tried to make you hate me. Then I tried to make people believe *I* hated *you*. There is so much shit going on that none of the current Heirs understand, and I thought I was protecting you from it. Instead, I handed you directly to that shithead Ramsey." He holds my gaze steadily, baring his pain and regret to me. "I'm sorry, Stella. What happened on Saturday night was my fault, and I will never let anything like that happen to you again, whether you can forgive me or not." My heart pounds, and my body tingles at the sincerity and emotion threaded through his words.

"I know you didn't mean what you said, and I also know that you had your reasons for saying it. Doesn't mean it didn't hurt like hell, though. You ripped my heart out and handed it to me, and in front of a roomful of people, no less." Stopping to organize my thoughts, I take a deep breath before my next words. "I'm choosing to forgive you. Please don't make me regret it. Things are going on in Folkestone I don't understand, things that have been in motion since before we were born, even I can sense that much. But I feel *alive* when I'm near you. Like I'm exactly where I'm supposed to be." My head dips slightly. "I feel whole for the first time in my life." His fingertips graze along my jaw and lift my chin.

"You have no idea how much I've wanted to hear you say that." My pulse pounds at the intensity behind his words. Searching my eyes briefly, he gives me a crooked little smile that melts my heart, and then proceeds to start the engine. "Are you okay if I make a quick stop before our drive?"

"Do what you need to do." Leaning back, I practically purr in appreciation as he pulls out onto the main road.

Holy shit, this is hands down the sexiest car my wrong side of the tracks ass has ever been in.

Running my hands over the soft red leather seat on either side of my thighs, I'm somehow transfixed by the smooth muscle in Poe's forearm as it tenses and releases when he changes gears.

"See something you like?" He asks in a teasing tone.

That's it, spaz, get caught by the hot guy, lusting over his arm. His fucking arm. God, you're such a weirdo.

"So, where are we going, anyway?" I ask, trying to distract him from my noticeable drooling.

"Just need to swing by my place for a second. There's something I want to grab." As he says it, he turns into a winding driveway, leading deep into the lush forest high on the point. A set of enormous gates, guarded by carved stone ravens, open slowly to allow us through. I try to be cool about it, but I'm pretty sure my shock at the size of the massive wood and glass house in front of us is written all over my face.

"This is your place? It's, uh, nice. Wow." Stumbling over my words, I stop talking altogether, and he gives me a wry laugh.

"Yeah, that pretty much sums up how I feel about it, too." Leaning over, he gives me the barest whisper of a kiss. "Wait here, beautiful, I'll be right back." Leaving the car running, he sprints to the dark wooden double doors and disappears inside.

Never mind fitting my New York apartment anywhere in this place, you could fit the entire damn building in it. Twice.

As my somewhat stunned gaze wanders over the expanse of glass along the front of the house, I notice the curtains twitch in an upstairs window, and a sharply beautiful but very pinched face stares back at me. I smile hesitantly, not sure if she can see me. She meets my eyes, and hate immediately floods her expression, giving me the willies.

Okay, so I guess she can see me.

The curtain falls back into place as the driver's side door opens and Poe climbs back in, stowing a small black bag at my feet.

"You okay? You look rattled." His brow creases in concern.

"Yeah, no, I'm good." I force a smile. "Where to now?"

CHAPTER TWENTY-ONE

*P*oe surprises me by driving us to the yacht club Spry and I passed when he first picked me up from the airport.

"You have a boat?" I ask with trepidation. Having never been on a boat of any kind, I'm nervous.

"My dad has a few. I want to show you my favorite." If he notices my nerves, he pretends not to and greets the valet by name as we pull up to the main building. Handing his keys to the kid with a handshake and a smile, he comes around to my side, opening the door and reaching in with his hand extended.

Here goes nothing.

I take his hand and let him pull me up out of my seat, feeling a little awkward in my school uniform. Grabbing the bag from the floor, he leads me down to the docks filled with everything from small speedboats to entire floating fiberglass palaces. I'm so busy looking at everything all at once, I almost crash into him as he stops next to a sleek, elegant, wooden craft.

"What do you think?" He asks hesitantly.

"It's beautiful," I breathe. The warm mahogany glows in the late afternoon sun and beckons me to run my hand over its smooth surface, so I happily oblige.

"Want to go for a ride?" His face lights up. Looking down at my school clothes, I squinch my face.

"I would love to, but I didn't really dress for it." Even though my nerves about being on a boat are still present, I'm also aware of an acute sense of disappointment.

"Why don't you let me worry about that? Come on, Star, come for a ride with me." He steps over the side and into the boat, turning back to look at me with a dare in his eyes.

How the hell does he already know that will work with me every time? Infuriating bastard.

Swallowing my fear, I stare right back at him as I step in and immediately stumble. He grins, catching me and pulling me against his chest. The rumble of laughter he doesn't even try to stifle has me swatting at him.

"I'm not laughing *at* you. I'm, well, no, I'm laughing at you." Shoving away from him, I cross my arms in front of me and try to look angry, but the happiness written all over his face and his relaxed movements make it impossible.

"Fine, I'll forgive you for this one, Halliday, but no more. You've used up all of your free passes." His glow is infectious, and soon I'm grinning right along with him.

Once we're ready to go, he starts the engines and directs me to the seat beside him. When he gets up to throw off the lines, it gives me a great view of his perfect ass.

Maybe I'm going to enjoy this, after all.

Smiling to myself, I settle back in my seat as he takes us out of the marina.

Once we hit open water, Poe takes me on a tour of the area, pointing out local landmarks and telling me stories of yachting with his dad. The boat we're on, he explains, is a thirty-three-foot Riva. This one is his favorite because all three Halliday men—grandfather, father, and son—used to take it out together, and it became their escape from real life for a few hours at a time. Listening to him talk about his grandfather and his dad, I can feel the love he has for both men radiating from him, and I'm content to sit and listen to the stories of his childhood, while we dawdle the afternoon away and lose track of time.

The sun is setting as he steers us back along the coast and around to the forested cliffs at the end of Folkestone Point, where a tiny secluded bay is carved into the rock. From this vantage point, the lights of the city are starting to twinkle in the distance off the bow, and the setting sun is a ball of fire in the west. Dropping anchor, Poe cuts the engines, and all I can hear is the water lapping against the sides of the boat.

"It's beautiful here."

"Don't sound so surprised. Did you think I was taking you somewhere awful?" He fakes a shocked expression with his hand over his heart.

"I had no idea what to think! First time on a boat, dick." Running my fingers through my windblown hair, I stick my tongue out at him.

"Oh, I'm sorry, were you talking to me?" Making a show of looking around for somebody else, he laughs as he reaches out and grabs me, pulling me out of my seat and into his lap. "There's no Dick here, sweetheart, only me. Poe Alexander Halliday. You'd better remember that."

"I don't know, it kinda feels like there's a dick here."

Snickering, I grind my hips playfully against him, watching as the spark of desire in his eyes ignites into a flame.

He lifts me easily, growling low in his throat as he carries me to the padded sunbed on the sloping aft deck and sets me down gently. I turn and face the stern of the boat, pulling my knees up to my chest and enjoying the soft breeze on my face. When I hear Lana Del Rey's 'West Coast' start to play quietly over the speakers spread throughout the boat, I smile.

"A little mood music, Halliday?" Teasing him, I look over my shoulder, and he takes my breath away, standing there barefoot in a white T-shirt and his gray school pants, the setting sun glinting off his rich dark hair and a wicked gleam in his eyes.

Why this incredible, gorgeous guy is looking at somebody like me as if I'm his last meal, I will never understand, but fuck if I'm not going to enjoy it.

The way his hands roam my skin, like a faithless man searching for meaning, moves me. It's not just erotic and sensual; it's profound. Nothing I've felt before has ever been so pure and so dirty at the same time.

"Your skin is the softest thing I've ever felt. So warm, so perfect." He murmurs against the side of my neck. His breath moves over a delicate spot near my ear and sends tiny, delicious waves of excitement pulsing through me.

My school clothes long gone, the nearly sheer material of my white bra rubs against my nipples, the sensation leaving them aching to be touched. Almost as if he read my mind, Poe's arm curls around my back, finding the clasp and opening it with deft fingers. His hand moves to my shoulder and slides the strap down my arm, exposing first one breast, then the other to the cool evening air. With a needy moan, I arch closer to him. Chuckling softly, he lowers his mouth to my nipple, swirling his tongue over the peak before sucking it between his teeth and biting lightly, mindful of the bruised skin surrounding it.

A gasp of pleasure escapes me, prompting him to continue his ministrations on to my other nipple, the piercing in his tongue both warm and cold, and his bite a little harder.

I'm writhing under the attention, wanting more, needing him to go further. To make me wholly his.

My fingers find the edge of his shirt, and he pauses long enough for me to tug it up over his head. The sight of his abs, paired with the V carving his hips disappearing into his low-slung waistband, has me hungry for him. Trailing one hand across his strong shoulder, I trace the sleeve tattoo I love so much down to its end at his wrist. Placing my hand on top of his and lacing our fingers together, I guide him to the warmth between my legs still covered by my panties and melt at the soft groan he can't hold back.

My free hand curves around the back of his neck, and I pull his mouth to mine, teasing him with the tip of my tongue and lightly tasting the shape of his lips while urging him on with our joined hands between my legs. Slipping aside the damp fabric of my panties, he untwines our fingers, and I release him, still not letting our lips fully touch. With a skill I appreciate, he slips his hand down my slit and slides his finger through my wetness, stroking my clit with a feather-light touch. My legs fall further apart to allow him better access and parting my lips, I kiss him hard as he pushes two fingers deep into me, and I rock into his hand without shame. Pulling his mouth away from mine, he moves to whisper in my ear.

"You are light in my darkness, Star."

The boat sways gently beneath us, adding to the weight-less feeling Poe is creating within me. He lifts himself off slightly, his fingers still playing with my wetness, and looks deep into my eyes.

"What do you want?" Such a vague question, with so many possible answers. But for me, there's only one.

"You." That single word, steady and sure, is the most honest thing I've ever felt. And he knows it. Not breaking eye contact, he slowly pulls his hand away. As I reach for the heavy black buckle on his belt, he licks both fingers that were inside me, a sexy grin on his beautiful mouth.

"I was hoping you'd say that." He gets to his feet, bare and planted wide on the aft deck, and stands shirtless and strong in the last of the evening light, the faint breeze ruffling his espresso hair and turning my nipples to hard points again. Never have I seen anything as commanding of attention and respect as the beautiful boy in front of me right now. The boy who is devouring every inch of me with his hungry gaze, silently worshipping the curve of my lips, my breasts, my hips.

His eyes still on me, I sit up and carefully get to my knees in front of him, my naked breasts heavy with desire. Finishing what I started with his belt, I move to his pants, undoing them and pushing them down the hard, toned length of his legs. Stepping out of them, he bends at the waist and lifts my chin for a brief kiss before gently pushing me down on my back again.

Dipping into the pocket of his discarded chinos, he pulls out a blue foil packet and slips it between his teeth, shim-mying out of his black boxer briefs. Taking the condom from him, I tuck it in the waistband of my panties and lift my hand to his now rock-hard cock. The feeling of the silken skin against my palm is incredible and has both of us breathing heavily as I tighten my grip and stroke his length.

"God, even your cock is amazing. You are spectacular in every way." Whispering the words under my breath, my cheeks heat when he chuckles, and I realize he heard me.

"Don't go getting embarrassed on me now, gorgeous." With a devilishly charming smirk riding his infinitely kissable lips, he hooks each of his forefingers under the sides of my panties and slides them off me while I tear open the condom wrapper and hold it ready for him. "What, you're going to make me dress myself?" he jokes lightly. Taking it from my fingers, he slowly rolls it over his length, putting on a bit of a show for me.

Sliding his perfect hands under the creamy skin of my thighs, he pushes my knees back and apart, exposing my center to him. Visibly shaking with the need to have him inside me, I tilt my hips upwards and say his name with every ounce of longing I can manage.

"Poe," I whimper. "Please." That's all it takes. With one hard thrust, he's buried in me as far as he can go. Holding still for a few seconds and giving my body time to adjust, he tucks a strand of hair behind my ear and gives me the most vulnerable smile.

"I don't want to hurt you, Star. Your bruises..." I lift my mouth to his, sealing our lips together, and twine my fingers in his thick hair. As our tongues tangle, he begins to move within me, resting one powerful forearm beside my head while the other stays under my thigh, pushing it higher. His thrusts take on the rhythm of the water beneath us, and I feel the release building in me at record speed.

Breaking our kiss, I tilt my head back against the cushioned deck and arch my neck in abandon. Seeing it as a perfect opportunity for a taste, he runs his teeth delicately along the straining length, nipping lightly at my earlobe. Feeling his movements quickening along with my own, the wave gets higher and higher until it crests and nearly drowns me in pure ecstasy.

"I'm—oh, God, Poe!" My nails dig into his shoulders as the orgasm rips through me like lightning, and I feel his deep answering groan as he pounds hard and deep three more times and comes with me.

When we finally find our voices again, he rests his forehead against mine, his thick dark lashes fanning against his tanned skin as he closes his eyes.

"Star, that was..." he flounders for the words.

"Perfect," I finish for him, lifting my chin and brushing a soft kiss across his lips before breaking into a grin. "It's nice to see you at a loss for words for a change," I tease. Tickling my sides briefly and giving me a mock stern look, he gets up carefully to dispose of the condom. Returning from the small cabin below deck with a cold beer, a bottle of water, and a blanket, he hands me the drinks as I sit up. He settles in behind me, both of us still naked, and wraps the blanket around us, pulling me back against his chest.

The burnt orange and red edges of the sunset the only light remaining in the sky, the approaching darkness and the movement of the boat lull me into a peace I don't think I've ever felt before.

"Thanks for the water," I say, reaching back to hand him the beer. Ignoring the beer, he grabs the water bottle and starts guzzling it. Wiping his mouth, he grins at me.

"Beer is for you, champ. I need to rehydrate after that workout." The laughter he's trying to hold in vibrates his chest against my bare back.

Two can play at that game.

Shrugging, I twist the top off the beer bottle and chug half of it.

"Whoa whoa whoa! I was kidding! Gimme that!" Full-on laughing now, he pulls the cold green glass bottle from my hand and replaces it with the clear plastic one. "Tradesies. Drink your water. *You* need to rehydrate for round two."

Pretending to be shocked, I elbow him in the side.

"And what makes you think there's going to be a round two, Halliday?"

"Because I make your toes curl, Bradleigh." He growls into my ear.

Do you ever.

Settling back into him as he rests his chin against the side of my head, the two of us finish our drinks in comfortable silence, watching the stars slowly twinkle to life in the velvet of the night sky. The absolute intimacy of sitting with him like this makes me feel whole and safe and protected. He sighs, and his voice is soft against my hair.

"For the record, I've never felt like this before, Star." He pauses and sighs. "I've never needed anybody, until you."

Feeling tears prick behind my eyes, I turn in his lap to face him and run my thumbs over the angles of his jaw.

"I need you too, Poe Alexander Halliday." The pad of his thumb is gentle as he runs it over my bottom lip, and he leans in to kiss me until my breathing starts to quicken again. He hardens against my thigh, and as I wrap my hand around him and slowly stroke him to near-panting, my mouth slides next to his ear. "This is the first time we've been intimate that hasn't involved a bathroom."

"Funny you should mention that. There's a tiny one in the cabin below deck. You interested?" He wiggles his eyebrows suggestively, and we both start laughing before he pushes me onto my back again and starts to kiss his way down my stomach, stopping just above my pubic bone. "No more bathrooms, Star. No more hiding how I feel about you from anybody." With that, the flat of his tongue finds my clit and starts working me toward my second orgasm of the night.

CHAPTER TWENTY-TWO

STELLA

*L*ying here, cuddled up in a blanket with Poe, curled against his side and floating under the stars, is heaven. My entire body is relaxed and soft, the comfort so sweet I don't ever want to leave it.

"Star?" The way he says his nickname for me like it's made of honey and sin, sends delicious shivers across my skin just as much as the fingers he runs over my shoulder and down my back.

"Hmmmm?" I murmur back, not wanting to break whatever magic is woven around us quite yet.

"Can I show you something?"

"I think you've already shown me plenty, but if you feel the need to show me again, I suppose I can live with that." Smiling against his chest, I slide my hand over the dips and planes of his abs, and down to the smooth skin of his already hardening cock. A hum of pleasure escapes him as he presses his face into my hair.

"Yes. So much yes, you naughty girl." Moving my head to get a better angle, I playfully bite his nipple and grin at his sharp intake of breath. "But first, I really do want to show you something." My curiosity is piqued by the subtle seriousness in his tone, and I push up on one elbow.

"What is it? Is something wrong?"

"No, not wrong. There's something I think you should have." Sitting up, he kisses my forehead gently before slipping out of our makeshift bed and padding over to his black bag in the cockpit. Watching him move smoothly through the moonlight with complete confidence is an incredibly intoxicating experience for me. When he turns back toward me, an envelope and a small LED lantern clutched in his hand, he catches me staring. Wearing nothing but a sexy little grin, he plays up his swagger on his way back to our little nest, stopping to pose a few times and making me laugh.

"You need to do that more often. Laugh, I mean. I swear to God, it's one of the sexiest sounds I've ever heard, all throaty and rich." He climbs back in beside me and nuzzles the side of my neck.

"*One* of the sexiest sounds? What are the others, and who do they belong to?" I give him my best scowling face, and that makes him chuckle.

"They're all you, no need to get jealous." He winks, and I snort. "What? Don't believe me? There's that sound you make when the stud in my tongue catches your nipple just right." He tugs the blanket down to demonstrate. "Then, there's the other one that happens when I slip my finger between your pussy lips, just before I circle your clit." Clamping my hand over my mouth, I clench my teeth and try in vain to avoid making any sound at all as he does precisely what he described. "Oh, and then there's my favorite one; the way my name sounds when you moan it just as you start to come." His voice is a low purr, and when he talks like this, I can't think about anything except how much I crave him. Shoving his face away playfully, I pull the blanket back up and swat at his roving hand.

"You said you wanted to show me something, so show me, Halliday."

"Fine." He pouts. "You're no fun."

"You know exactly how much fun I am, jackass. If you ever want to experience it again, get on with the show-and-tell, already." My threat is complete bullshit, but he pretends to take it seriously and sits up beside me.

"So obviously somebody has explained some of the history of this town to you because you know about the Heirs." I nod, and he continues. "My dad came home early from a business trip. He never comes home early, and he's rarely there at all anymore." He pauses. "I think he came back because of you." He runs his hand through his dark hair, leaving bits of it standing in tousled, spiky disarray.

"Because of me? He's never even heard of me." A chill races across my naked flesh that has nothing to do with the air temperature, but Poe notices and goes back to his black bag. Pulling two hoodies and a pair of joggers from it, he stops to flick on the low interior lighting and retrieves our underwear on his way back.

Grateful he thought to throw some clothes into his bag when we stopped at his place earlier, I pull on the soft white sweatshirt he hands me, burying my nose in the fabric briefly to inhale his scent and watch as he gets dressed. Blatantly ogling him while he slips into his black boxer briefs, I'm wholly stunned this gorgeous human wants to be with *me*.

"Stop looking at me like that, Bradleigh, or those panties you've just put on are coming right back off again." He licks his lips, and I roll my eyes. His response is to throw his joggers at my head, and I catch them with ease. "Put those on so you stop being so fucking tempting." I quickly wiggle into them, cinch the drawstring, and fold the waistband down a couple of times to keep them up. Poe slides his school pants back on and comes to sit cross-legged next to me. He studies me in silence for a minute like he's committing every inch of my face to memory.

"Poe, you're starting to freak me out a little. What's going on?" I start nibbling on my left thumbnail.

"I'm pretty sure my dad has heard of you. Or at least the abstract idea of you." He hands me the greeting card-sized envelope.

Did it have to be another envelope? The only thing better than an envelope at turning my life inside out and upside down is a box. He better not have a fucking box hidden around here somewhere.

Taking a deep breath to push back the creeping panic, I open the unsealed back flap and pull out a photo. Angling it slightly to see it better in the light of the lantern, I immediately recognize my mother, about my age, and holding the hand of a boy who looks an awful lot like Poe.

"What is this?" I squint at the details in the picture. "Are those the front steps at Woodington? Is that your *dad?*"

"It's all of our parents, one for each of us. The Heirs from the generation before us."

I'm too shocked to speak, and suddenly the quiet around us is broken by the opening chords of 'Season of The Flood' by Alexisonfire—Payne's chosen ringtone that he also happily associated with his number on my own phone. Poe gets up to answer it, leaving me to stare at my mother, young and happy, none of the fear or sadness I watched her carry reflected in her eyes.

"Star, we have to go. Now." In a frenzy, Poe grabs for my hand, taking the photo from me in the process and planting me solidly in the seat next to the wheel. Stuffing the blanket and the lantern back in the bag, along with my school uniform and his button-down, he carefully tucks the picture of our parents in between the folds of my school shirt and tugs on his hoodie. Seeing the fear written plainly on my face, he quickly leans in and kisses me once, hard, on the lips.

Weighing anchor, he fires the engines to life, and we roar back to the marina, the wind whipping the tears from my eyes before they have a chance to fall.

Once back at the yacht club, he quickly ties the lines and practically drags me off the boat, pulling me down the dock behind him by one hand, while I try to slip my shoes on with the other without actually stopping. My foot tangles in the extra length of Poe's joggers, and I trip, falling on my ass and wrenching my hand from his grip. Swiping at my frustrated tears with the back of my hand, I tug my shoes on and roll onto my hands and knees to push myself up.

Everything goes sideways as I stare unblinkingly at the stern of the Halliday family boat.

"Poe?" I ask, my voice barely above a whisper.

"Star, come on. I'm sorry, beautiful, but we have to go." He comes back to me and reaches down to pull me to my feet. I resist and try my voice again.

"Poe." Something in my voice stops him.

"What? Come on. What's the matter?" This time I let him pull me up, and I swing my eyes to his, pointing with my free arm at the elegant script on the stern.

"Why is your boat named 'Evangeline'?" My teeth clench against the vomit rising in my throat.

"What?" He looks confused for a split second like he can't figure out what I'm asking him. "Evangeline was my grandmother—my dad's mom." I can feel all the blood drain from my face, inch by inch, as I slowly step back from Poe.

"Star? What the hell? Are you okay? You don't look so good." He takes a step toward me, and I take another one back. "Star?" Tears stream down my cheeks, hot and bitter.

"My middle name is Evangeline. That photo of our parents." My throat burns. "Are we...?" The surprise that registers on his face when he hears that tidbit of information is real, that much I'm sure of.

"Really?" The corners of his mouth turn up in a small, thoughtful smile. "My grandparents would have liked you a lot," he muses.

"Halliday!" I all but yell. "What in the holy fuck is going on? Answer my question, or I'm not going anywhere with you. Ever!" The wind kicks up off the water, making the boats moored around us bob and sway, almost as if in support of my stance. Tilting his head back and taking a deep breath, he's silent for a few seconds before returning his focus on me.

"No. We aren't." At those words, relief floods through me, and I feel like I can swallow again. "The night my dad came home, the same night he gave me that photo, he also voiced his approval of you and me. The next morning, he encouraged me to make it right with you, and not to let anybody come between us." He takes a step forward, and this time I don't retreat. Grabbing both of my hands, he holds them tightly between us, locking his eyes with mine. "He wouldn't have done that if there was even a chance that we..." I nod, accepting his logic. "I'll tell you everything else I know, but we really need to go, so can we please go get the damn car now?"

★

By the time we get to the valet and the car is pulled around, another ten minutes pass, and Poe's restless anxiety is amplifying my own. Once we're on the road, flying down the dark streets, I realize we're heading back toward his place.

"Spill it. What's going on?" Glancing at my phone, I see it's almost eleven o'clock. "It's late, Poe. What did Payne say?"

"Honestly, I don't know why they decided to do this now." He takes the turn into his driveway fast and sharp, rocking me against the passenger door, and brakes hard in front of his house. The first thing I notice is the number of cars parked in the area next to the massive garage; the second is how many of them I recognize.

Sunday's Rover.

Raff's new Porsche.

My aunt's Cadillac.

My aunt's Cadillac?

Some people get hangry, but me? I get pangry. When I start getting a little too freaked out, the panic bleeds into anger, and it tends to make me yell. And cuss. A lot.

"Halliday!" I bark. "Why is my aunt at your fucking house? Why are the other Heirs here? Is this some kind of a lynch mob? Because it feels a little late on a school night for a goddamn party!" My chest rising and falling quickly with my shallow breaths, I fling open my door and jump out, ready to punch some motherfuckers in the head if I need to.

Shaking his head and laughing under his breath, Poe gets out and comes around to my side of the car.

"Has anybody ever told you you're sexy as hell when you're pissed, Bradleigh?" Seething silence is my only response, and he quickly realizes that I'm not fucking around. "Okay, here's the deal," he says soberly. "Payne called to tell me to get you here. There was a meeting about the Heirs tonight, which wasn't unexpected. You're back now, so our parents, and your aunt, need to make sure all their little chess pieces are where they're supposed to be. My father mentioned earlier that he wanted to have you formally introduced as the Bradleigh Heir as soon as possible. It would have been nice if he mentioned it was going to be *tonight,* though." He rolls his shoulders to loosen some of his own tension. "What *is* unexpected is that the Torstens are here. If this meeting is about the Heirs, they have no stake in the game. Payne said they're causing some kind of shit, and we needed to get back here."

"The Torstens? As in Hali?" My brows raise in surprise.

"Yeah." Reaching out, he threads his fingers through mine and lifts our joined hands to his lips, kissing my knuckles softly. "You ready for this, killer?" He asks with a wink.

"Probably not, but what the hell. Let's go." Squeezing his hand tightly, I follow him straight into my nightmare.

CHAPTER TWENTY-THREE

The scene that greets us in the formal living room of Poe's large glass and wood house can only be described as controlled chaos, voices all talking over each other. Tightening my grip on his hand, I let him lead me into the room, and the effect our arrival has on the occupants inside is immediate.

Sunday and the girls get up, and each gives me a big hug, Sunday attaching herself to my left side and hooking her arm through mine. The guys get up to join Poe, Raff dropping a kiss on my head as he walks in front of me.

"Sun, this is weird," I say in hushed tones. "Should I be afraid? Why are you guys all here?" She hugs my arm tighter to her side briefly but doesn't answer me, reluctantly letting go as she backs up slightly to stand with Roxy and Aylie, leaving Poe and I front and center. Poe stands strong and tall beside me, his thumb softly rubbing slow circles in my palm in a small, but emotionally intimate gesture that makes my heart squeeze.

Scanning the adults in the room, I recognize bits of my friends' faces in their respective parents, and I see my aunt standing with a man who looks so much like Poe, it can only be his father. The welcoming smiles on most of the faces, as well as Cecily's proud beaming one, all help me feel slightly less like I'm standing in front of a firing squad.

The elder Halliday leans down to say something to Cecily that has her cutting her bright blue-green eyes to the woman I just now notice standing slightly behind the large main group.

The woman in the window.

A martini glass filled with something resembling dirty dishwater is clutched in her red-tipped claws. With her is Hali, her hatred for me darkening her pretty features and twisting her lips into an ugly shape, and two other people I can only assume are Mr. and Mrs. Torsten.

The woman is small and elegantly beautiful but nervous and hesitant, sitting with her hands folded carefully in her lap. Her slight head tilt allows her hair to fall forward and partially obscure her face, and her shoulders hunch forward in a self-protective way.

I know that position well; I grew up with it.

If she dared to look me in the eyes, the fear written in hers would echo my mother's.

The man standing just in front of her exudes a cruel arrogance, and she subtly flinches every time he moves. Everything from the harsh slash of his thin lips, to his small eyes, set just a little too closely together, screams for attention. Right now, those beady little fucking eyes are roving over me with a familiarity that makes me want to take a shower, but I raise my chin and stare back defiantly.

All of a sudden, I remember that I'm standing in front of these people for the very first time, in what are obviously not my own clothes, hair windblown, and wearing next to no makeup, most of which had been rubbed off during sexy times on the boat.

Oh my God. Can everybody tell we just had sex? Do I have 'I just had a toe-curling orgasm! Ask me how!' written all over my face?

Feeling my cheeks heat with embarrassment, I'm just about to ask Poe where the nearest bathroom is when his father and Cecily approach us.

"Thanks for coming home for this. We wanted to introduce Stella to everybody tonight. How are you, son?" He clasps Poe's shoulder in greeting, and takes a sip of his scotch, the caramel-tinted liquid rolling smoothly in the short glass. "Payne mentioned you took Stella here out on the Riva this afternoon. Did you two have fun?" Father and son both seem to be having a tough time keeping a straight face right now, their eyes twinkling, and the corners of their mouths twitching almost in unison.

Oh yeah. He knows EXACTLY what happened this afternoon. Well, that's fucking mortifying, isn't it?

Squeezing my now sweaty palm, almost like he can feel my need to bolt from this shitshow, Poe allows his face to break into a grin.

"Dad, I'd like you to meet Stella Bradleigh. My girlfriend." I look up at him in surprise, and he smiles insolently down at me, almost daring me to challenge his statement. Rolling my eyes, I look back to his father with a bold smile.

"It's nice to meet you, Mr. Halliday. You must be the one with both the brains and the looks in the family. Your son may be pretty, but he clearly lacks in smarts as he's just announced that I'm his girlfriend without first asking me if I'm interested in the position." Poe's father roars with laughter, and my aunt coughs delicately to cover her snicker.

"You're not wrong, Stella," he jokes. Holding out a hand for me to shake, a wash of sadness passes over his handsome face briefly before he manages to tuck it away again. "Please, call me Holt. And I have to say, you remind me so much of your mother. It's a pleasure to meet you."

"Thank you, sir. I'm happy to meet you as well." Holt's deep blue eyes, so much like his son's, show nothing but warmth and kindness, and I realize my statement is more than a platitude; I *am* happy to meet him. He's a link to a side of my mother I never had the chance to know, and I'm hoping he'll share some of their history with me.

Cecily leans in and hugs me tightly, smoothing down my hair, and carefully examining my face for the truth.

"You okay with this one now?" She jerks her head in the younger Halliday's direction, making Holt and I both chuckle. Nodding, I squeeze Poe's hand.

"Poe, I think you know my aunt, Cecily Bradleigh? Auntie, this is Poe Halliday. My boyfriend." He snorts.

"Oh, sure, it's okay for *you* to announce things without asking. What if *I'm* not interested in the position?" Able to hold a straight face for all of eleven and a half seconds, he finally quits trying. "Who am I kidding? Of course, I'm interested. That position is all mine." He gives me a tight side-hug before leaning forward and kissing my aunt on the cheek. "Hi, Miss B. It's good to see you again. To see you *here*."

Before I can ask where else they saw each other, a sharp voice dripping with cold venom cuts through the pleasant chatter in the room.

"While all of this is just so *nice*, there's a bit of a problem here." Callum Torsten slinks forward, hands clasped behind his back. "I've been promised certain things, and the Halliday spawn is set to marry my Harriet."

Leaning into Poe, I whisper to his shoulder, "Who the hell is Harriet, and since when are you supposed to marry her?"

"Hali is short for Harriet." Unable to entirely swallow my laugh, I try to cover it with a cough.

Yeah, that bitch isn't getting anywhere near Poe, no matter what her name is.

Callum swings his shifty gaze to land on me.

"So, this little fling between him and the Bradleigh whore will be ending immediately."

Both Poe and his father snap their heads around at his use of the word *whore*.

"I'll have you keep a civil tongue in your mouth while you're in my home, Torsten. You will not speak of *any* woman here that way." He advances toward Callum. "There are no promises regarding our children. Poe and Stella are free to be together." Holt Halliday has at least five inches on the Torsten patriarch, but that doesn't seem to deter the smaller man from pushing into Mr. Halliday's personal space.

"Perhaps we should ask your wife, Holt." His cruel mouth thins even further. "Eunice, darling, be a dear and get the fuck over here *now*." Eunice Halliday looks like she would rather drown in her dirty martini than face the room full of people staring at her with a mixture of curiosity and disdain, but Callum has effectively removed any other option for her.

Wobbling slightly as she crosses to stand beside him, she still manages to look mean as a snake when she leans in and hisses in his ear.

"Callum, discretion, please. This is not the time or the place." With a hateful squawk of perverse laughter, Callum shakes his head.

"Oh, we're long past the point of discretion, Eunice. The minute that trash set foot in Folkestone and was not only allowed to stay, but was *welcomed*, it was only a matter of time before your sins came to light."

"*My* sins? You had a pretty heavy hand in this too, Callum. You don't think there will be a reckoning for *you*?" Poe's mother's face is growing paler by the minute as she tries in vain to figure out a way to reroute this conversation.

My stomach starts doing somersaults as panic's dark wings unfold around me.

Something awful is about to happen.

Going against everything my brain is telling me to do, I stand my ground and pray that I'm wrong.

"I think one of you had better tell me what the hell is going on. Obviously, Callum believes he is owed something, Eunice, and I'm very interested to learn what it is and what exactly *you* got in return." Holt's clipped tone is frigid and leaves no room for defiance.

The room around us is silent; the air strained and thick with tension as we all wait for the bomb to drop. Even Hali looks less sure of herself than usual. Cecily moves a little closer to me and takes my free hand.

"Do you want to tell them, Eunice? Do you want to tell them what happened to the Bradleigh Heir, to their precious Catherine?"

The entire gathering gasps as one, and the bottom drops out of my stomach.

Holt takes a threatening step closer to Callum, the rocks glass in his hand in danger of being squeezed to death.

"What did you just say?" He asks, his body vibrating and voice rigid with anger.

"I remember how badly you wanted Holt back then, Eunice." Callum's voice takes on a psychotic, sing-song pitch. Like somebody who knows he's fucked, and is going to take as many others down with him as he can. "You were obsessed, and he was promised to the Bradleigh bitch. Worse than that, he loved her." My tears flow freely as he spits the words like little poison darts. "Did you get off on watching them fuck when you would follow them and hide in the shadows?" I gag, and Poe wraps his arm tightly around my shoulders as Cecily nearly crushes my hand in hers. "You tried everything to get his attention, and he ignored you. They all ignored you. You weren't one of the Heirs; you were nothing. Just a pretty face with a daddy who had something old man Halliday wanted. Until the night everything changed."

Eunice Halliday bares her teeth in a feral snarl. Her drink forgotten, I watch the liquid slosh onto the soft, steel blue carpet in slow motion as she drops her martini glass.

"Shut up, Callum. Just shut your fucking mouth for once in your miserable life!" She clenches her hands at her sides.

"*My* miserable life? What about poor Catherine's misery?" He sneers my mother's name with the disdain of a jilted lover, and I want nothing more than to punch his veneered teeth down his throat. "At least I got to fuck her once, though, even if she did fight me the entire time. I owe you a big thanks for that, Eunice. If you hadn't convinced her that Holt wanted to meet out at the old barn on his grandfather's property, I never would have had my chance."

The blood pounding in my ears does nothing to dampen the roar that erupts from Poe's father as he launches himself directly at Callum's throat. Eunice tries to take a step back, to disappear into the shadows again, but Raff and Payne block her as they circle behind her.

The men in the room race to separate Holt's hands from Callum's neck before he outright snaps it, while the women turn to help Cecily who looks like she's going to pass out any second.

From the corner of my eye, I see Sunday slip out of the room when Callum's high-pitched crazy cuts through the noise.

"Eunice promised she'd find a way into the Heirs, and that she'd take me with her, and she did. Poe and Harriet were promised to each other the minute they were born." He laughs maniacally. "I would've broken Catherine for free, though. That self-righteous cunt deserved everything she got in that barn. Beating her within an inch of her life and then fucking her bloody was the best night of my life."

The barn. The barn. The old barn. My mother. Me.

Realization slams home, and my throat threatens to close.

Poe lunges after his father as the older man struggles to break free of the grip Heller's and Payne's dads have on him. The pain and grief pouring off Holt Halliday are drowning him. Drowning *me.*

Standing silently in the chaotic sea of Callum's revelations, my eyes are drawn to Mrs. Torsten. Sitting and staring straight at me, the horror and resolve on her lovely face are an apology her mouth can never speak, her tears mirroring my own. Slowly she stands, moving unnoticed by anyone but me, to Eunice's discarded drink lying on the carpet. With her eyes focused on her half-choked and wholly evil husband, she picks up the martini glass and somehow snaps the stem off. With bloody hands, she calmly and deliberately walks to Callum's side and jams the jagged end deep into the fleshy part of his neck, right beneath his jaw. Pulling it back out, she drops it at his feet before returning to her chair.

Hali starts screaming, followed by some of the other

216

women in the room. Raff and Heller are holding Eunice upright, and I think she might have passed out at the sight of the bright red blood spurting from the sucking wound. Cecily looks like she's going to vomit, but pauses long enough on her way out of the room to spit in Callum's face.

Something about watching another Bradleigh do that to another Torsten forces a sick sort of laughter from my throat. I feel numb and disconnected, like the scene playing out in front of me is happening to somebody else, and I'm watching dispassionately from the sidelines as her life crumbles again.

Slipping from the room, I walk silently to the front door, paying no attention to the voice calling my name behind me.

Sunday's waiting in her Rover. When she sees me, she reaches over and throws open the passenger side door.

"Get in," she says quietly. Emotionless and exhausted, I climb in. Pulling the door closed behind me, I lean my head against the side window in time to watch in the side-view mirror as Poe runs out the front door. "Where to?" Sunday questions as she pulls away, leaving the beautiful, bloodied boy yelling after us. Turning away from my heartbreak, I look at my best friend's worried face.

"Ever been to New York?"

PLAYLISTS

Fragile Things - Stella's Playlist
Available on Spotify

'West Coast' - Lana Del Rey
'Never' - Terranova
'Waiting for the Night' - Depeche Mode
'Drama Free' - deadmau5 feat. Lights
'Renegade' - The Anix
'Take Me Down' - The Pretty Reckless
'We Don't Have to Dance' - ACTORS
'Teach Me To Fight' - YONAKA
'Closer' - Kings of Leon
'Feral Roots' - Rival Sons
'Last Resort & Spa' - Battle Tapes
'Change My Mind' - Silent Rival
'After Night' - MXMS
'Saturnalia' - Marilyn Manson
'Demon' - Tusks
'Gravedigger' - MXMS
'I Will Stay' - Flux Pavillion, Turin Brakes

'Feel Nothing' - HEALTH

Fragile Things - Poe's Playlist
Available on Spotify

'Just Got Wicked' - Cold
'Nutshell' - Alice In Chains
'Riot!' - Arrested Youth
'Careless' - The Blue Stones
'Stupid Girl' - Cold
'My Name Is Human' - Highly Suspect
'MANTRA' - Bring Me The Horizon
'Summertime' - Yellow Claw, San Holo
'Lips Like Morphine' - Kill Hannah
'Blurry' - Puddle of Mud
'Lay' - The Blue Stones
'Pain' - Bilmuri
'Antisocialist' - Asking Alexandria
'Bloodline' - Northlane
'Yellowbox' - The Neighbourhood
'Alibi' - Mansionair
'Can Your Hear Me' - Korn
'Youngest Daughter' - Superheaven
'Limbo' - Salem
'Heavier' - Slaves
'Pariah' - alt.

ACKNOWLEDGMENTS

Well. Here we are. I had so much fun writing Fragile Things and I can't wait to delve deeper in the mysteries of Folkestone Sins in book two, Fractured Things.

I honestly can't believe I finally did it, and I sure as hell didn't do it alone.

Steph, my wonderful alpha and friend, thank you for your unwavering support, both emotionally and physically (how many people can I legit say THAT to?), right from the night I told you and Brent, over chicken wings and beer, that I was going to do this crazy thing. You are my sister from another mister and I love you to bits.

Brandi. Where do I even start? Meeting you changed the game. Editor, PA, shrink, kindred spirit. I would be neither published nor sane without you. Your friendship means the world to me and I can't wait to see how much trouble we can get into. You're stuck with me forever now.

Siobhan, the tiny Spitfire. Thank you for all of your hard work and the kicks in the arse from across the pond.

My betas! Gina, Sonal, Annah, Erin, Amber, and

Mercedes - you guys are the best. Thank you for giving up your valuable time to help an unknown author get her first book published.

Cassie, thank you for the beautiful cover, for listening to me ramble on about everything and nothing, and for giving me some of the best advice and recommendations I've gotten on this journey so far.

Shales, you're the bomb. You make it all so damn pretty and I'm so looking forward to the next batch.

Rumi, thank you for catching what the rest of us missed. I apologize for not warning you about the damn spaces. Poe and Stella and I will do better on the next one.

Mel, thank you for introducing me to the amazing group of people I'm working with. I am truly grateful beyond words.

To all of the amazing authors I've met, your encouragement, advice, and kindness have been overwhelming. Thank you for being an inspiration, each and every one of you.

Boo Radley, I would need a whole book in and of itself to thank you for everything, so I'll keep it short and sweet. For every 'I'll be there in a minute' that turned into hours, every peanut butter toast dinner, every panic attack, thank you for taking it in stride. You've been my rock and I am so thankful for everything you are and everything you do. Winnie and I love you very much. Side note - looks like I finally managed to snag your last name. ;)

Mum. Thank you for instilling a love of books and music in me when I was tiny. Both are such a huge part of the fabric of my soul and that's all you. And fast cars. Oh, and English muffins on Christmas Eve. Rescuing animals. Smoked salmon brunches. Cribbage. The list goes on. You taught me I could do anything I wanted to, so I did. And here we are. I love you.

To all of my friends and family, thank you for your support, your love, and your tolerance of me being forgetful and absent.

To my readers, thank you for taking a chance on me. I promise, the best is yet to come.

Now Available

Read the next book in Stella and Poe's story

Fractured Things (Folkestone Sins Book Two)

Coming Soon - Preorder Available Now

Look for the beginning of Sunday and Payne's story, coming February 2021

Restless Things (Folkestone Sins Book Three)

.

ABOUT THE AUTHOR

Samantha Lovelock is a sarcastic individual with a decent sense of humour, darknesses hidden in mind-closets that occasionally Jack-in-The-Box her unsuspecting ass, and a love and loyalty for her friends and family that runs deeper than any ocean. Her guy means the world to her, and so does her cat; sometimes even in that order. Her Mum is her hero, hands down. She proudly wears the crown of a Queen of Innuendo, and of Name That Tune, and has never met a cliffhanger she didn't like. She lives in the foothills of the Canadian Rockies with her British cowboy and their Norwegian Forest Cat, Winston Churchill.

f facebook.com/samanthalovelockwrites
🐦 twitter.com/authorslovelock
📷 instagram.com/authorsamanthalovelock
BB bookbub.com/profile/samantha-lovelock
g goodreads.com/samanthalovelock